Dear Midge

Dear Midge

ROY C. WUNSCH

iUniverse, Inc.
Bloomington

Dear Midge

This is a work of fiction. All of the characters, names, incidents, organizations, and dialogue in this novel are either the products of the author's imagination or are used fictitiously.

iUniverse books may be ordered through booksellers or by contacting:

iUniverse
1663 Liberty Drive
Bloomington, IN 47403
www.iuniverse.com
1-800-Authors (1-800-288-4677)

Because of the dynamic nature of the Internet, any web addresses or links contained in this book may have changed since publication and may no longer be valid. The views expressed in this work are solely those of the author and do not necessarily reflect the views of the publisher, and the publisher hereby disclaims any responsibility for them.

Any people depicted in stock imagery provided by Thinkstock are models, and such images are being used for illustrative purposes only.

Certain stock imagery © Thinkstock.

ISBN: 978-1-4620-6507-3 (sc)
ISBN: 978-1-4620-6506-6 (e)
ISBN: 978-1-4620-6508-0 (dj)

Library of Congress Control Number: 2011960046

Printed in the United States of America

iUniverse rev. date: 11/14/2011

For
Mom, Dad, and Cindy
To those who have inspired me and have given me hope and
a gentle nudge throughout this creative journey, I say thank
you. To those people, places, and things I have drawn from to
make the book a reality, I am forever in your debt.

Don't be afraid of being unique. It's like being afraid
of your best self.

—*Donald Trump*

Dear Midge,

I could not help but remember the fun we had with you and Reggie on the cruise to the Yucatan. Lord, honey, if the walls on that ship could talk, we would be in trouble. You and that sense of humor and tongue and the way we ate our way through Mexico, I am surprised we made it to land without the boat sinking. Congratulations on your weight loss. The fat flush really seems to have worked wonders on you. Now if the both of us could quit smoking. I am tempted to try hypnosis. You should join me. Here is the news about my most recent adventure.

Stucky and I just returned from a wonderful guided tour of Rome we took with several of our friends and other parishioners from our church, St. Sally of Sweden. We departed out of St. Louis and connected through Seattle, where we met up with a sister church from that area. They are members of a progressive church called Christ the King Jesuit Jubilation.

Once we arrived in Rome, we were met at the airport by our tour guide Adina and boarded a bus bound for our hotel in the Caesarean section of Rome. After such an unusually long flight, we had the afternoon to rest and get acquainted with our surroundings before a lovely group meal at a quaint neighborhood restaurant called Saucy Sal's. Authentic Italian cuisine—magnifico! A walking tour with Adina followed our meal.

Tuesday morning we hit the ground hard. Well not me, but Stucky did fall out of the bed. After a speedy continental breakfast of mostly cheese, sausage, and fruit, we boarded our coach and headed to some of the spectacular Old

World areas of Rome. First we visited a factory where they make Communion wafers. Midge, did you know those come in a variety of flavors? The red velvet was my favorite. We also had a stopover at the expansive St. Paul Mall, where we found amazing Euro fashions, religious vestment knockoffs, and every Roman souvenir imaginable. Sena and Carlos Speermander were with us, and she picked up a stunning hat to wear to her next Red Hat meeting. It is done almost entirely of mosaic tiles.

Our next stop included lunch at the famed Ravioli Rastafarian Retreat. They were lined up around the block, but of course, our group had a reservation. Such a unique experience, and the food was outstanding. I had the toasted ravioli with pesto and the special herbal seasoning. Stucky had the flank steak marinara with the winter herbs. Lunch was just what we needed. We were rejuvenated for the remainder of the day and had a pleasant pep in our step.

The afternoon was on our own, followed by a lovely evening meal at Sabatino's. All-you-can-eat crab legs and pasta. A dream come true for all of us.

Wednesday we toured ancient Rome, which was so rich in history, as if my kids' schoolbooks had come alive.

Thursday was our day at the Vatican. You could almost feel the heart palpitations of everyone as we crossed into the city. Adina gave us a history of the square and Basilica itself. We had a phenomenal tour of the great hall and the awe-inspiring Sistine Chapel. We toured the museums, the grotto, and the gardens and had much of the day to explore. After a day of beauty and faith, I did not think things could get any better until we arrived for dinner at the acclaimed Rosaryta's Trattoria. It is famous for its flaming tomato pies and the rainbow tortellini with jumbo meatballs. Most of the wait staff dressed up in traditional Italian pomp and circumstance attire, and it is so festive.

On our final day, we did some mission outreach, going in to the streets of Rome and passing out literature about our Catholic faith and trying to convert as many of the locals to visit the holy church. This portion of the trip was clearly not well thought out but had merit if we were visiting another part of the world. We heard many times over again, "Stupid Americani," which loosely translates to "Stupid Americans." And then I heard "Chi ti ha detto che si guarda bene in pantaloni stretch," which I've come to find out is "Who told you that you look good in stretch pants?" So I came away a little more educated about Roman customs and found out that I should save my stretch pants for our trip to Brazil.

Midge, I hope that you and Reggie will consider one of St. Sally's upcoming guided tours. In the fall of next year, we are going to Rio de Janeiro, and then the following spring we are going to see the Great Wall of China. That last one is just a slide show, but maybe one day we will get there.

See you soon,
Jeanelle Vandusen

Dear Midge,

I am writing to solicit your help with the forty-third and a half Annual Afton Early Spring Winter Carnival. This year's theme is Ice Is Bloomin' All Around. Midge, this year virtually all of Afton will be converted to a winter wonderland. Sally John Hereford is already harvesting icicles, and Racine Redementer has received a truckload of ice blocks to turn her ranch-style home on Milford Avenue into an igloo.

The Culinary Institute of Afton will host the spectacular ice-sculpting competition. This year, contestants will pair off in twos to adhere to the Ice Is Twice as Nice motif of the carnival.

Snavely's Snow Cones is creating a special pickles-and-peaches snow cone, and Diddle's Dairy Dip will feature sundaes in many of their local favorites, including Wine and Dandy with Fermented Grapes, Lentils and Cream, and the flavor of the month—Honey-Glazed Ham Cookie Dough.

Top Tee is having a miniature golf tournament with an Alaskan theme, complete with a salmon-spawning pond, and Afton West Tech is putting the finishing touches on a cross-country skiing path through Main Street.

Hector Johnson at the Afton Aztec Museum is sponsoring this year's Miss Winter Carnival. Monique Mistadt, last year's queen, will crown the winner; and I am hoping you will be one of the distinguished judges, Midge. Do you remember when we were contestants all those years ago? Not only will the contestants have to compete in talent, evening gown, and snowsuit competitions but they will also be required to build an anatomically correct snowman while blindfolded.

Should make for an entertaining finale to a wonderful carnival.

Midge, I know you are working part-time for ASLUT, but I hope we can count on your assistance for our festival.

Thanks and see you soon.
Magenta Snipplewell

~~~~~~

Dear Midge,

I could hardly wait to write to you and tell you about our recent trip to The Holy Cross Mega Church and Resort in Boilingrock. The place is amazing, and when the weekend ended, Clarence and I did not want to leave.

We arrived on Wednesday and had tickets to the production of *How Wise Is Your Man*. It was a hilarious look at the length men go to in order to get out of going to church. It was followed by a midnight cruise along the lake aboard the *Noah's Ark II*.

Thursday we met up with Florine and Bobo Dunwoody. We had decided months ago to make this trip, so we all made reservations at the Loaves and Fishes Couples Retreat on the campus of the mega church. They have a wonderful four-star restaurant called the Last Supper, where we had a marvelous meal of The Lord is My Shepherd's Pie. A culinary masterpiece.

Friday was shopping day at the resort, and boy, did we make a dent. Florine and I headed over to the Crown Of Thorns Hat Shop, and each walked away with several goodies. We then headed over to the Mary Magdalene Lingerie Shop, where we tried on several things but just couldn't bring ourselves to buy anything. I think I may kick myself for that someday. Finally we stopped in at the How Great Thou Art gift shop. I stocked up on some gifts including, the Twelve Disciples monthly calendar. They look so different in designer duds. While I was busy browsing, Florine hit the jackpot. Turns out there is a bit of gambling going on here, and Florine won fifty dollars in the slot machine at the store.

Friday evening we went to game night at the recreation center at the resort. We played several games of Solitaire for Sinners and Bible Bingo. We had a lot of fun. Afterward, we headed to the Cup Runeth Over Coffee Shop and Ice Cream Parlor. I had the Sacramental Sherbet, and Clarence had the colossal Ten Commandments Sundae with ten scoops of ice cream. I have no idea where he puts it all.

It was a wonderful weekend with good friends, and we are already planning our next visit. Clarence and I are planning to renew our wedding vows for our twenty-fifth anniversary. We are going to come back to Holy Cross and celebrate at the Divine Mysteries Wedding Chapel and Banquet Center. We hope you and Reggie will join us.

All my best, Midge,
Euphonia Carbridge

Dear Midge,

I love this time of year. The season of Lent brings out so many things that are wonderful, but I especially love the fish fries that so many of the churches hold throughout the season. Herlene Cromsky, Abigail Schnot, Peolo Nordet, and I have formed the Cod Squad and have made it a mission to find the best fish fry around.

We were at St. Margaret Queen of Peace Parish and had a wonderful catfish dinner. I had the fish filets, pickled beets, and Norwegian black sheep slaw. The other girls had the jack salmon special. They are very predictable.

The following week, we chose VFW no.365 and then had a wonderful spread of broiled fish, seafood salad, and canned tuna. Interesting side dishes included Jell-O salad with carrots, candied cucumbers, three-bean salad with way too many wax beans, and, finally, macaroni and cheese made with angel-hair pasta.

Week number three found us at the Mexican fish fry at St. Joseph the Greater Church in the city. It was a lively and festive concoction of traditional fish fry favorites along with treats from south of the border. We had tuna casserole tacos and nachos with orange roughy. As we mixed and mingled, there was entertainment to be had. The children from some of the creative arts classes, dressed in authentic Mexican attire, sang and danced; and as a finale, the fourth-grade class, dressed as burritos, paid tribute to the world-famous mariachi band, Saulo Horhay and the Sombrero Midgets.

Week four brought us to the Chilargo Fire Department in Denton County. They had a fantastic dinner with imitation crab and farmer's sushi, which is really just a fancy term for deviled eggs with caviar.

Week five was a tribute to the international fish market in Soulard. We had French carp fillets and German Flaukenshider, which is similar to rainbow trout except it is sweet and sour. We also had an Irish fish stew made with gingered shark meat and beer.

Finally as the Lenten season drew to a close, we finished our tour with a stop at St. Cletus of Germania and the traditional sea bass tartar buffet at St. Marvela the Anguished in Arnold.

Midge, I hope you will consider joining the Cod Squad next year as we search for the best fish fry in the metro area.

Easter tidings,
Qualine Loinstar

Dear Midge,

You really made a fantastic showing at the spring carnival with your famous chow chow. Congratulations on winning first place in the pickle relish and chow chow division.

Hansel Hoverzilly looked stunned when his chocolate chow chow did not take the top prize again this year. He went from milk chocolate to dark, and I think that is what cost him.

I was so happy to see little Simone—well, actually, big Simone now—entering the annual rug-hooking category. She is becoming quite good. I have no doubt she'll break into the top ten next year. She is obviously a good hooker.

Did I hear correctly that Reggie caught so many bass in the fishing tournament that they had to restock the tank? I guess his experience on the shrimp boat gives him the upper hand.

Irene Irsky and Louise Lively-Lutz put on brave faces after they lost out to Cynthia Cordmier in the table-setting contest. With ten kids, I guess Cynthia takes the cake. I think she selected the red velvet that Gonquila Gordez made from scratch.

Midge, job well done on the chow chow.

Sooner rather than later, we need to get together for lunch.

Till then,
Perky Patterson

Dear Midge,

I am writing to you to ask for your help once again this year at the Jesse James School's annual Taco Bar Bonanza and Spanish Festival. As parent moderator of the fifth-grade class, I am recruiting other parents to assist in making this the best bonanza possible.

This year's theme is Ole in May and will be held as usual on the day of the celebration of Cinco de Mayo. I think it would be an injustice if I did not ask you to bring a big vat of your famous seven-layer dip. It always seems to be such a hit. You are so coy about what you add to give it that extra zing. You must share the recipe, and I can add it the school bulletin.

We are asking each parent to contribute five dollars to purchase suckers and other hard candy, along with trinkets for the piñata challenge. This year promises to be exciting, as the art department has worked hard to create a piñata that resembles Principal Morris.

Remember to also bring a baked good for the cakewalk, and be sure to sell lots of raffle tickets. We are so lucky that Mrs. Clark's home ec department has made a map of Mexico using scraps of fabric, old buttons, and dried beans and macaroni noodles. A treasure for the winner, I am sure.

Anyway, Midge, I know we can count on your support as usual. We look forward to seeing you and the whole family on May 5. Remember to wear your favorite Spanish-themed outfit, as there is a twenty-five-dollar gift certificate from the Honey Hut for most original costume.

Sincerely,

Bev Richards-Taylor
Parent Moderator

Dear Midge,

This morning I went to the neighborhood association meeting at the home of Atula and Eldon Amatulli. She mentioned that you and Reggie were having new carpet installed in your bonus room. Now that the kids are a little older, there is probably not a need for all that indoor-outdoor carpet. We discussed the giant pyramid of shrubbery in front of Rutger and Rachelle Rotenbaum's two-story home. Midge, you know how they are, and the neighbors are a little concerned that if we allow one thing to happen, it will turn in to a horticultural amusement park.

It was also decided that the Afton Town Council would charge a fine of twenty-five cents for any dog doodling in other neighbors' yards. They ask that you clean up after your pet.

Sandy Sue Siebert asked all neighbors to bring old newspapers to her house, as the recycle bins are now there. They moved them from the curbside so that the mailman would stop running over them.

Finally, Pollard and Paula P'Neal have asked for prayers this week for their cat Scrumptious, who was recently hospitalized after she ate a pound and a half of deli meat from Dilly's Deli. The olive loaf must have fallen from Paula's grocery bag after running errands last Tuesday.

Prayers were also requested for Glynn Olhausen, who recently chipped a tooth while eating fried spam.

Midge, we hope to see you and Reggie at the next neighborhood association meeting on the twenty-third.

Bye for now,
Juanita Moosavi

Dear Midge,

Rodman and Tita Shrobak send their regards. They remembered you and Reggie from last year's annual smelt soiree. They remarked at what fabulous dancers you both were. I reminded them that you both had lessons from Elmer Analovich over at Dancin' in the Streets ballroom and two-stepping classes.

The smelt soiree this year will be held at the posh Afton Club. One of the highlights, no doubt, will be Dorine Danoid and her flock of dancing poodles. I heard that they also got Francoise Fendergrass to come in from Fenton to sing a melody of fish songs.

I've been shopping for weeks to find a new dress. The selection has been poor, and then I went over to Clayton and found the Ritzy Rag. Midge, the selection was amazing, and I found a stunning black cocktail dress with starfish and sea monkeys done in jewels right at the bust line. It is so glamorous and I feel like a queen.

Listen, girl, we hope to see you both there next Saturday.

Regards,
Peggy Poteete

Dear Midge,

Thank you for sending me your recipe for your famous seven-layer dip. I had no idea that the fifth layer was butterscotch pudding.

Today I went to the White Sale at Garrison's Grocer-rama, bait and tackle beauty parlor.

That nice man, Eugene Garrison, put all the white products at 10 percent off. I loaded up on milk, eggs, bread, cottage cheese, bar soap, laundry detergent, rice, and cauliflower.

I wish you could have been there to get some of Reggie's favorite ranch dressing.

While there I had a rinse and set from my beautician, Geraldine. She does such a wonderful job keeping my roots from showing. She sets it and teases it, and I wrap in all up in toilet paper before bed.

Sweetie, I am off to the Puttin Pad. Shalandria Owenstein has turned me on to a dear little sport called putt-putt.

Love ya tons,
Georganna

Dear Midge,

Well tonight was just grand. Sonny and I enjoyed our night out with you and Reggie. I know he does not get home much, as this is high season on the shrimp boats, and we are so glad you both chose to honor us with our dinner invitation.

Uncle Mandrell's is such a great place, and Sonny and I love it so. I was surprised to hear you and Reggie had never been there.

The chopped sirloin salad Reggie and Sonny both had looked amazing, as well as the jumbo shrimp cocktail. Reggie sure knows his crustaceans. I think they are far better than those at Merv Maryville's Tavern.

I am so glad you went with the hamburger steak and apple bacon coleslaw. It is certainly one of my favorites. I went with my old standby chicken tenderlits and home fries. My figure hates it, but it is so good.

Sonny and Reggie sure enjoyed telling war stories of their days at Reginald Pewster High School over in Ladue. Along with Homer Hubert, they were the three musketeers with their rowdy shenanigans.

Midge, thank you again for your company and friendship. We must do it again soon.

Porter's Pancakes & Pigs' Feet just opened in Plantersville, and we've being dying to try it.

Love to you,
Lerner Lasckleman

Dear Midge,

Ermantrue Lampe here. Hope you're doing well. I wanted to tell you that I am hosting a fifty-fourth birthday celebration for Ms. Minerva Mollyson.

The party will be at my house, which is at 6464 Octillo Drive. You will remember it well from our Parcheesi parties. I do love to entertain.

I thought I would do a luncheon in honor of Minerva and thought the theme would be trashy and tacky costumes of the fifties.

Minerva has always enjoyed the eccentric side of fashion, so this should be right up her alley.

I've asked her brother Hubert Mollyson to be in on the surprise, and he will drop her off at around eleven thirty. I am asking guests to arrive at eleven and suggest you ride with Edna Rae because parking is at a premium.

I suggest a small gift of cash for the money tree or a little token of your esteem. You know how Minerva loves a hat. She often calls out, "Today is a say-something hat day."

Would you mind terribly if I asked you to bring your wonderfully delicious deviled eggs? They are always a hit and so pretty with all the edible glitter.

Looking forward to the big day.

Fondly,
Ermantrue

Dear Midge,

Thank you for giving me the name and number of your gout specialist.

Dr. Dillard Dandridge was kind enough to fit me in on Thursday to check out my gout. It flared up again last Sunday while I was at my sister's celebrating the birthday of her little grandbaby, Cleveland.

Cleveland is a picky little tot and only eats barbecue ribs, okra, and dill pickles; so the buffet at the party was less than desirable. But the cake was lovely. German chocolate innards with cream cheese frosting. On the top of the cake was a miniature train set with the words, "Happy Birthday, Clevey."

Dolly Dolley-Downy was over last week to show off her new cat. She named it Curly. It is apparent the cat has straight hairs, so I am not sure from where the name is derived. Further, this poor cat looks like it has done nothing more that walk into doors. It has one of those smooshed-in faces and squinty eyes. Poor dear.

Freddie Foster is once again doing lawn care for me. He does a wonderful job, and my bushes have never looked lovelier.

Love you dear,
Martha Murray Moobley

Dear Midge,

How are you? I feel like it's been a blue moon since we last saw you and Reggie at the neighborhood July 4 chili cook-off. I still have fond memories of your delicious concoction made with ground polish sausage, bratwurst, and hot dogs. It reminded me of the beanie-weenie soup my mother used to make.

Anyway, Donna Bonnie had me over to give me an update on the drama department's annual musical. This year they are doing a musical version of the film *Independence Day.*

The art department has been busy making sets of the White House, New York City, and some military installations. They have also made some fabulous sets depicting the UFOs and aliens, although some of the actors will also double as aliens with costumes made of foam. We are hoping that Reggie Jr. will consider one of these nonspeaking roles.

I learned that Tibby Tooney will play the lead role as president, and there is a number of speaking roles as well as plenty of extras. It will be interesting to see how this all plays out.

Sheryl Shepard Shearson is in the hospital over at St. Mary's. She suffered what she thought was a stroke, but in fact, it is a virus that causes temporary facial paralysis. Her mouth is drawn, and she is drooling on herself but has remained in good form considering. Having a conversation is difficult; thank goodness we both know some sign language. Keep her in your prayers.

I need to run. I am working on music for the singing roles and dance numbers in the school musical.

Darling, talk soon for sure.
Nancy Neiderland

~~~~~~

Dear Midge,

Dear, how are you? I wanted to take time to write you and thank you for the lovely hanging plant you sent when my cousin Hollins passed away. Your thoughtfulness was much appreciated.

As you know Hollins died in a rare kangaroo attack while visiting Australia. He and his wife, Wilda, were there along with Wilda's sister Tilda and her husband, Foster.

They were at the kangaroo farm near Perth and were visiting an area where the animals were close enough to pet through a liberally fenced-in area. Hollins dropped the camera behind the fence and reached all the way through the fence to retrieve it. When the baby popped out of the pouch and grabbed the camera and hopped back in the pouch again, Hollins leaped over the fence and charged after the 'roo.

The 'roo cornered Hollins and began to beat him with his feet. Yes, you heard me correctly, Midge. Hollins was kangaroo-thumped to death.

Poor Wilda just watched in horror. When they returned home, Wilda promptly destroyed her entire collection of kangaroo novelty figurines from their travels. One of the main reasons for going to Australia was to add more figurines to her collection.

Now that she is adapting to life without her beloved Hollins, she told me she's switching to collecting pig figures and plans to tour much of the Midwest's hog farm gift shops to build up this collection.

This is just great. Next time I have to visit her home there will be a bunch of porkers staring at me through a curio cabinet.

Anyway, thanks for your thoughtful expression of sympathy.

Love,
Maudine and Kenson Beauregard

~~~~~~

Dear Midge,

Hi, it is Candy Cooley from over at Seventh Avenue Savings and Loan Co., South Needland branch. As you know, we are offering a lovely set of china when you open a Christmas Club account. This year we've welcomed back one of our most popular patterns called Cherry Blossom in June. It is truly spectacular.

In years past, you have always opened a Christmas account, and my goodness, you must have almost every china set we have ever offered. At my count, that must be around fifteen—plus all the various pots, pans, and serving pieces. Where in heavens do you go with it all?

Edna Rae came in last week to open her Xmas account, and from the looks of it, she must be planning on a big holiday.

Cornelia Cottenwoods from over in Guthrie was in earlier this week and told me what fun you ladies have been having in the Red Hat Society. It must be so much fun parading about town in your purple dresses and red hats.

I would not know, as I hate purple. Actually, anything flavored grape as well. Just turns my stomach—*yuck!* I can't even begin to think about it. But I am sure you all have fun anyway.

Midge, I hope we'll be seeing you soon to deposit into this year's seasonal fund. It's never too early to get the ball rolling.

Cordially,
Candy

Dear Midge,

Thank you for agreeing to be a judge in this year's March Marzipan and Music Festival. The art of marzipan is so intriguing, and this year marks Afton's tenth anniversary celebration. In years past, we have had every likeness of political figures, entertainers, an array of fruit, and many special-themed entries. This year will be something special.

Categories include Best Use of Marzipan, Most Original Design, Best Likeness of Dolly Parton, Best Use of Marzipan for Household Decoration, and Best Holiday Theme. As you will recall from last year, Estelle Willows and Shirl Hampede won best in show with their entry titled Summer Picnic. I was truly amazed that they included a three-bean salad and ants on top of a picnic table in such detail. They have had a lock on first place for the last few years, but this year promises new and exciting challengers.

Four brothers from England have been granted admission to our little festival, and they promise to give Estelle and Shirl a run for their money. Barclay, Bentley, Bernie, and Byron Brantsford are the reigning titleholders in England and have won many top prizes here in the States. I for one am anxious to see their entry. Last year in Odessa, Texas, they won the top prize by designing an entire dinner party, including the guests. Many attendees to the exhibit thought the food was real and said they could almost smell the prime rib.

It should be a contest like no other.

Midge, I need to run. Abu, the African foreign exchange

student staying with us, is doing his daily tribal chant; and the dogs are going crazy.

Thank you again, and see you at the festival.
Zelda Greenbladt

~~~~~~

Midge,

How are you? It seems like it takes a note to really catch up even though we talk all the time. I seem to be taking on more responsibilities with each passing hour and never seem to have a moment to myself.

I took a few personal days from my job at the Quick Cash Station and decided to give you a speedy update and elaborate on some of the things we talked about the other day.

Wayne is doing well, and with his recent promotion at the plant, we can finally afford to get some new drapes and pay off the expenses from Mary Jane's wedding. It is approaching sooner than we think. I believe I finally found a dress. After looking all over Watsonville, I had to drive in to Clarkson, and it was at Silky and Shiny Boutique. Midge, it is beautiful. I never dreamed that a fuller-figure woman of substance could look so good in lavender chiffon, but this dress really hides the extra pounds I can't seem to get rid of. It has a hat with feathers, and I think I am going to splurge and get it. Wayne is going to wear his gray tux from the shrine. It is a little tight, but by April, he should be okay. We are laying off sweets.

Matt is enjoying playing the tuba in the high school marching band. He is so much smaller than the other kids, but he hoists that tuba high and proud and does a great job. Mary Jane asked him to be an usher in the wedding, and he is so excited.

Mom and Dad are doing well and looking forward to coming to visit for the wedding. They don't get here much anymore.

It takes them a month of Sundays to pack, and I swear they bring everything they own. If the fridge can fit into Dad's old wagon, he'd bring it along. Last time, they forgot Mom's medicine, and just getting them through that was a treat if you recall. It is just easier if we go up to Maple Valley and see them.

My Bunco group is off and running. How is yours doing? Each week we take turns hosting at one another's house. I am hoping Hildy and I can find a third player soon.

Anyway, let's talk in a day or two, and we cannot wait to see you and Reggie at Mary Jane's big day. Thank you so much for hosting a shower. She was so excited with all the lovely gifts. Don't forget about the rehearsal dinner. Doug's parents are hosting at Royal Oak Tavern. It is such a classy place.

Tootles,
Edna Rae

~~~~~~

Dear Midge,

I was recently at the home of Cleopatra Goldfarb, and we were making baskets for the children's home run by Hestor and Jimmy Wayne Nesbit. We annually get together and make baskets to let the children know we are thinking about them

We were joined by Agnes Wexly, Sandy Sue Silverman, and Molly Moeler. Cleo had a wonderful buffet of snacks, including pickled herring tartlets, sweet potato wontons, pigs in a blanket, and cheese curls, next to which she had a bowl of clothespins. She uses these to pick up the cheese curls so that her guests do not get orange fingers. I thought this was a fabulous idea.

We loaded up our baskets with gym socks, number-two pencils, a can of tennis balls, deodorant, peanut-butter crackers, four dozens of hard-boiled eggs, and some wax fruit. We changed things up a bit this year and hope the kids will like it.

Sandy Sue was telling us that her husband, Archie, has become quite the shopper of the As Seen on TV products. His sleep pattern is off, and he is usually up late watching mindless television and somehow manages to buy something new every couple of days.

She was saying that just last week he bought the Dynamo Milker, which makes milking cows a breeze. Am I the only one who thinks this is an odd choice since they live in an apartment and have no cows? He also got the Sterling Silver Q-Tip Dispenser. He opted to have that one engraved with the family crest.

Molly Moeler was telling us about her recent trip to Ireland. She could not believe how beautiful it was and that they had their very own Billy's Burger Bar. She bought several souvenirs and considers the authentic Irish tam made from bay leaves and cocktail straws to be her favorite keepsake from the trip.

Jack Todd and I are going to our niece Bertrice's wedding in Tuba, Wisconsin, on Friday. We are renting a stretch limo station wagon and taking the kids. Jack Todd's aunt Verla is coming along. We had to put our foot down and tell her she could not bring her dog, Mr. Diddles. He tends to make the kids nervous, and he is allergic to water and only drinks Tang.

I will be sure to show you the photos when we see you and Reggie at the ballpark for Skip Noostead's Annual Softball and Slingshot Spectacular.

All the best, Midge,
Clarice Juksaw

Dear Midge Clovis,

As president of ASLUT, I am writing today to ask for your support and, more so, your efforts in spreading the good news and fantastic benefits of our organization. ASLUT (American Society of Ladies' Unmentionables and Toys) relies heavily on dedicated members like you to spread the good word. Many of our products, including motivational tapes, lingerie, lotions, potions, and stimulating trinkets, are found right there in the average house in Afton.

Your community of friends and supporters, the parties you have hosted, and the conventions you have attended go a long way in furthering our mission: to make every woman in America ASLUT.

Enclosed with this letter, please find our newest ASLUT bumper sticker and window decal. You will also find your new membership card as well as a free sample of one of our newest lotions. Osage Sapling is a new lotion product we are testing, and we hope to hear back from you with positive feedback. We hope this small token will encourage your efforts, and we hope we can rely on your continued support in the coming year.

Remember, we need each member to recruit six new members this year, and we look forward to seeing you and all the members at our yearly conference in Spawn Lake, Iowa.

Thank you for being such a loyal member of our group. We need more women like you to become ASLUT this year.

Sincerely,
Bruno McKnight
President
ASLUT

~~~~~~

~~~~~~

Dear Midge,

After months of searching for a solution to Clyde's baldness, we found a great local place—Dangling Threads Hair Replacement Center of South Afton. We are so thrilled. He can finally start to phase out those horrid hairpieces. The place that Reggie referred us to was booked up to almost a year.

After the army, where he was forced to wear a helmet, he came back looking like he'd been wearing a bowl on his head.

Midge, have I got some juicy news. Kiki Kilmer was at the club on Saturday. Wearing one of her midriff-bearing tops naturally, I noticed from afar a dark spot on her lower stomach. Well curiosity got the best of me. I meandered over to her and struck up a conversation. It was clear to me that Kiki had a tattoo.

I was caught off guard that she had taken such a step to permanently alter her body even with what looked to be a small square shape. Yes, Midge, you heard correctly. She has the outline of a square on her mid section.

I asked her what the square was, and she said it was Iowa. Midge, that damn fool has the state of Iowa stamped on her abdomen. She is from Davenport after all, so that lessens the shock slightly.

If I were putting a state on my body, I'd go for something like Florida. That way, with bad vision, some folks would think I was being a little naughty.

Like I've always said, Afton is home to a variety of weird people. But aren't most towns.

Listen, darling, I have to get over to Iris Panozzo's, as today we're making hand-painted and bejeweled planters for the annual Shruberry Stampede in Dalton.

Sincerely,
Lorraine Lustfeldt

Dear Midge,

Hope this note finds you well after your recent outing at the Afton Zoo. I heard that they had to remove a couple of monkeys from the ape exhibit for showing their special no-no places to the public. I think they're calling it indecent exposure.

My thoughts on this, Midge, is that the monkeys should be wearing clothing if they are having so much trouble with monkey masturbation.

As you know, Henning and I have been separated since I caught him cheating with Carol Carson-Capson. I have decided his sorry ass is not worth fighting for, so I am filing for divorce.

I went to see the four-brother law firm Newhauser, Newhauser, Newhauser & Kline for representation. I am using Nipsy Newhauser. I am asking for sole custody of the children, the house and both cars, as well as all his fishing stuff and favorite baseball glove.

Midge, I am off to the Good Egg to pick up a dozen or so.

Talk to you real, real soon,
Poodle Pinkersly

Dear Midge,

Your success with the Fenton Freelance Latino Guild prompted me to get involved in the community and wanted to give you an update.

As you know I am an honorary member of the Afton Asian American Society. I guess those frequent meals at Shin Loo's Noodle Rodeo really paid off. At last week's meeting it was decided that there is an immediate need for a regional Asian online dating service. I am delighted to announce that the site went live last night—Woo Got Mail, where you can search for Mr. Right or Ms. Wong. Love is in the air.

We also decided that this year's annual fundraising event would be a 5k walk/run to benefit the Sunny Cho Center for Fortune Cookie Culinary Arts at the Afton Technical Institute. This year we are hoping to fund scholarships for one girl and one boy to attend the two-year program. Sam Ng from the Cape Girardeau Chopstick Theatre will be the honorary chairman for this year's event. The Great Green Tea Race will not soon be forgotten.

On Friday evening before the race, the Afton Asian American Society will hold a magnificent prerace gala with a performance from the prestigious chopstick theatre troupe. They have put together a remarkable piece entitled, *To Soy with Love*. There will be additional entertainment provided by ASS (Asian Singing Sailors) and Sandra Chueng, the soloist with the Chinese Bird Ballet. She will be doing her parakeet pirouette routine with thirty-six feathered friends.

This is an exciting time for cultural events in our area, Midge, and I look forward to seeing you and Reggie front and center.

Love to you and the kids,
Erlinda Gooseberry

Dear Midge,

Well today we celebrated the graduation of our niece Carlene from the Holstead College of Dietary Arts. We also took time to celebrate the twenty-fifth wedding anniversary of Winston's sister and brother-in-law, Benita and Barry Boinkin. It was a wonderful day, and we hosted the party at our home and managed to keep much of the festivities in the backyard.

We set up buffet tables on the patio and served an array of lunch meats, pasta salad, pistachio pudding, Uncle Al's German potato salad, Aunt JuJu's multilayer salad, deviled eggs, and the like. We had a big cake from Zolfinger's Bakery. It read, "Congratulations on Your Graduation and 25 Years of Wedded Bliss."

All the kids played badminton and chased our dog, Squirt, around the yard for hours. All was good till ole Squirt dropped dead right near Auntie Purtle. She dropped her cake and ran and fell over one of the little ones and sprained her wrist. She was screaming in pain, the dog was dead, cake on the ground, and little Maliki was eating the cake off the grass.

Ned and Oscar agreed to take Auntie Purtle to the minute clinic for an x-ray, and several others helped us move the dog to the garage until Winston could get a hole dug. As you remember, it was just last year when Cooper's pet turtle tried climbing up the basement steps and got its neck caught on a loose carpet fiber and hung itself. We are not doing so well on the house pet thing.

Anyway, I wanted to thank you for sending over the casserole for our company. The eggplant and pineapple succotash was a huge hit, and I must get your recipe.

Many thanks for coming to my aid, Midge, and I will see you at Bunco soon.

Teresa Tidberry

~~~~~~

Dear Midge,

I returned Thursday from a week in Springfield with the Literary Society of Greater Mid-America and the Northern Territories of the Ozarks and attended Camdenton's annual Book Bedazzle. It was a truly amazing week of great books, talented authors, and an array of new and enchanted stories that are sure to become classics in the years to come. Midge, with your flair for the written word and your quick wit, you should consider writing a book.

One of my favorites at the Bazaar was *There's a Catfish in the Closet*. It is a unique story about a puppet and his owner and the relationship they forge when they visit with a beauty school professor. It really has nothing to do with a catfish or a closet, but I thought the title was cute.

Another standout was *A Parrot for Petunia*. It is a precious story about the bonding friendship between a young little girl and her dear parrot. They became best pals and actually secret confidants. Little Petunia often shared her innermost secrets with the bird, and as the two grew older, more and more secrets were revealed. One day while Petunia was at stenography school, the parrot started yapping and yapping and yapping while Petunia's mom was listening. It turns out that among the secrets that Petunia had shared with the parrot was that she had been dating the young Baxter boy even though she had been forbidden to see him by her parents. Well, when Petunia found out the bird blabbed, Petunia acted harshly. The sequel to the book is called *A Possum for Petunia*.

As I walked through the various tents with my friend Arnie (You may remember that he was married to my best friend

Nonie until she was killed at the Martinsville Crawdad Carnival. He and I were always close and have been dating for about a year. My husband Clifford is clueless), we discovered several booths with homemade bookmarks, book covers, book lights, and bookends. Arnie bought a nice set with the likeness of Niagara Falls on them. They are truly spectacular.

To close out the week, we attended the final book read. This year a bright new author read excerpts from her book, *Dixie Mabel: My Life as a Transsexual Beauty Queen*. She was the Cornhusk Queen of Trenton, New Jersey. It is a fascinating tale of betrayal, as she was beaten out for Miss New Jersey by a buxom blonde who we later learned had stuffed her bra to gain points from one of the judges nicknamed "Like 'em Large Luther." A panel had determined the judge acted inappropriately but that the contestant earned enough points in all her categories to actually win. Devastated, Dixie Mabel ended up being a red-carpet correspondent for a cable access channel.

We are planning to go back next year, and I am hoping to take a larger group and stay a few extra days and take in the sights of Springfield. The annual tour of famous back alleys is the same week, and that seems like something I would be interested in seeing. Can we count you in?

Talk soon,
Roxanne Walker-Trotts

Dear Midge,

Clarence and I are taking off in a few days for a much-needed vacation with the kids. We will join my sister LaDonna and her husband, Buck, and their three for a week at Rimwood Lodge. It is a great place nestled among pines near Elm River in Lewiston. We go every year, and this is a great family place where Mom and Dad took my siblings and me, and many of our other relations joined us as well.

We will stay in adjoining cabins with LaDonna, Buck, and the kids, who will have lots of activities to keep them busy. Shuffleboard and Jarts for the adults, and Lord knows Buck packs enough beer for a month, and you know how I love my whiskey sours.

We get three meals a day and eat with all the other families who are spending the week at Rimwood too. It is a great chance to rekindle old friendships. The highlight of the week will be the talent show and, of course, the water rodeo on Saturday. The adults usually stay up late playing cards after the little ones go to bed.

Last year was a lot of fun, and LaDonna's son Kev finally made it from the cabins to the pool without crying from the pain of wearing thongs. I think that little piece between the toes got the best of him. The kids always poked fun at him hobbling across the drive, dragging his sore feet like they were clubs.

One of my favorite things is always seeing the array of swimsuits the ladies wear. While inner tubing down the Elm River, we ladies sit in those inner tubes, and our thighs look all big and jelly filled. Some days I wish I could wear pants to avoid looking at my unsightly thunder thighs. All of the suits in my size seem to have attached skirts or gosh-awful ruffles on them, and they all seem to make me appear like I got off the special bus.

The kids spend hours on the river catching crawdads and other little water animals and keep them alive in poorly made rock ponds. I am sure those little animals wish we never invaded their territory. My nephew Shim always seems to manage to kill most of the animals and crawdads because he handles them too much. I think it is his way of loving on them.

I hope maybe you and Reggie will consider coming with us one of these years.

I have to go. Clarence has the downstairs table covered with things he thinks we are taking on this trip. I have to go down there and show him that although his intensions are good, we are not taking a portable toilet or the canoe.

Bye, dear,
Narleene

Dear Midge,

I am beside myself as the annual church picnic approaches. I have been on the event planning committee, and we have an event that is going to be something special this year. It all kicks off on Saturday morning with the books of the Bible children's parade and carnival. This year each grade will ride on a different-themed float with the usual suspects, including Matthew, Mark, Luke, and John. The Psalms and Proverbs players will do various renditions of the most popular Bible stories.

We have planned a wonderful carnival with lots of booths and games. One of my favorites is Fire and Brimstones, where fire shoots out of boxes and the kids will use water guns to put out the flames. This year we have added a new feature. The Lord is My Shepherd Petting Zoo will feature a variety of animals for the kids to get up close and personal with.

I am also looking forward to the Miss Old Testament Pageant. It will be tough to top last year's winner, Polly Pat Williams, who has given so generously of her time while serving food to the shut-ins, volunteering at the Ladies' Auxiliary Pancake Social and lecturing about her new book, *100 Ways to Give Your Cell Block a Designer Makeover*, down at the Smithfield County Detention Center. In fact the other day I heard that one of the incarcerated men won a blue ribbon at the county arts and crafts festival for his macramé hanging planter. Midge, I hear his work is outstanding.

I plan to get to the picnic early, as Brother Donald and the Palm Sunday Singers will be singing selections from their new cassette, *Heaven's Just Two Flights Up*. I hope to stay to see the Last Supper display made of Popsicle sticks and twinkle lights.

I know we will all have some great fun. See you there.

Cathy Carlyle Cummings

Dear Midge,

I am so excited about some recent news I heard from Glenda Wenky. She was at the new strip center over in St. Charles and discovered a wonderful new place called Sushi and Smoothies. She said it was incredible.

She went with the Ladies' Luncheonettes, her women's group from church. They all had the Adam and Eve Roll, which used a fig leaf instead of seaweed, and a couple of the ladies tried the catfish and the orange roughy. They ended their feast with peach-and-prawn smoothies and said it was an ample serving.

Last month they tried the new all-you-can-eat restaurant over on Carver Avenue.

Little Luigi's Big Ole Buffet is not for the light eater. Mounds and mounds of mama's spaghetti and all the Italian feast you can handle. They all had the Leaning Tower of Pisa Salad Spectacular and Roman Coliseum Food Bar. Charlemagne Tillford said it was the best Italian food she has ever had.

I heard that next month they are traveling to Woodbury and dining at Rick's BBQ, where they will watch Rick pull his own pork shoulder. I hear his spicy sauce is the best in town.

I've got to tell you, Midge, I think we are missing out on this fabulous food fun. Maybe we should start our own lunch group, but with all the weight you have lost with the fat flush, you might be tempted by the rich and oh-so-fattening food.

See you soon,
Molly Longmire

Dear Midge,

Well, we missed seeing you and Reggie at the thirty-fifth anniversary celebration for Zander and Elya Morshower. Their children really threw a wonderful event at the Lion's Club. So many of their family from the old country came in, and friends from near and far were seated at tables around a dance floor.

Music was provided by the Willie Stinkles Tuba Trio, Conchetta and Ivan Marrow, The Duet Delight, and the all-alto choir from the Sisters of Salvation Ministry. Dancing was at your own risk.

A beautiful replica of their original wedding cake was on display. One of the cake servers tried to cut into it but quickly realized it was made of Styrofoam. The actual cake was a wonderful tiered confection with four separate layers—traditional white cake, red velvet, carrot cake, and the top layer was an iced Bundt cake with the bride and groom sitting on the center. It looked like they were actually popping out of the cake or sitting in a hot tub.

None other than Afton's own Guenella Holdstrom catered the afternoon meal. She really has a way with a buffet. She did carved ham, green beans, pickled beets, iceberg lettuce wedges, and twice-baked potatoes, although I think she actually bakes them three times.

Fruited tea and fruited coffee were also served with the meal and dessert.

A table was set aside for gifts. Cam and Tilda Isenstager and Thom and I gave a money tree that Tilda made at the art league. We tied dollar bills shaped like little birds all over the tree. I think we had seventeen of them. We got a little carried away with the birds after taking an origami class over at Nelson Valley High School.

The guests each took a small favor home. It was a picture of Zander and Elya when they got married printed on a little card and tied to a zip lock bag of Tic Tacs. It was a lovely memento of a fabulous evening.

On another note, Gladdy Thomas was there with her neighbor Sally Sue Edwards. Turns out Marvel was not able to attend, as he has a temporary sight problem from putting in a too-high-a-wattage bulb in one of the overhead lights and was overcome with the magnificent brightness. Others were all gossip, saying this was just her excuse, as he was away on another "extended" business trip.

Anyway, we sure missed you and hope to see you soon. By the way, Elya looked amazing since she dropped the three pounds.

Talk soon,
Kaliopee

Dear Midge,

So good of you to call last week and check on me after my fall at Johnson's Slapjack Junction. Maybe next time I'll know better than to overload on syrup. I always get a little too excited when they bring out all those flavored syrups. Mixing and matching should never be done on an empty stomach.

Wouldn't you know, half the town was dining out when I slipped and broke my leg. Mabeline Montgomery and the Captain were there along with Goebel and Frannie Flatbush, celebrating the recent announcement that LooSea Siff was taking over as president of the Banjo and Other Stringed Instrument Auxiliary Guild of Greater Afton. They were all toasting and cheering over a wonderful meal of silver-dollar slapjacks.

Brenda Jo Jankowitz and Trudy Stillmeyer were there planning the ladies' luncheon at the Moose Lodge. This year the theme is Got Moose? I am not sure what they are planning, but you can be sure the photo booth will look like a real masterpiece, as Trudy's husband, Milton, is a pro with a jigsaw.

Mary Pat Connor and Melowny Primweiser sent me an invitation to a baby shower for Donwella Smitter. She is expecting another child after all these years. For crying out loud, Midge, she is a grandma twice with her first child. That husband of hers never gives up.

Listen, Midge, there is so much more to write, but I have a chicken potpie in the oven, and I don't want my famous thistlewood crust to burn.

See you at the shower.
Maybelle

~~~~~~

Dear Midge,

Sweetie, I just got off the phone with Anita Manlee-Mann. She has been under the weather for weeks, and doctors just discovered that she has a rare condition. She has rhinoplastdaster, where her sinuses are somehow misconnected to her bladder. For years she has peed a little when she sneezes, and the poor dear has to wear adult diapers when she has a head cold. She is finally taking something for it, and my hope is that she will be feeling well enough to attend the fashion show of Dina Darnell.

I saw a preview of some of her creations last week, and I'm telling you she has a hit on her hands. Her primary collection is a glowing array of jumpsuits, caftans, and minidresses. Her use of felt squares as a textile is genius. She also uses burlap, satin, and camel hair; but these are used sparingly as to not draw attention from the fabulous felt squares.

It is perhaps her glamorous collection of accessories that will have everybody talking. Made up of oversized earrings from household cookie cutters, fabulous chokers designed from glittered rickrack, and amazing hairpieces made from the floral bathtub decals that we use to prevent slipping. They are back and more beautiful than ever.

An assortment of leg warmers, tube tops, and spandex bicycle shorts complete the festive looks—each one a distinctive masterpiece that only Dina can create.

She is doing a full runway show with models from Maxine's Modeling Museum. Hair will be by Ham's Heavenly Coiffeur and makeup by Gino from Glow Glam Squad.

I am so excited and look forward to seeing you and all the other ladies for a day of festive fashions.

Fondly,
Nan Nunley

~~~~~~

Dear Midge,

Garnett Gilispie and I just got back from Sally Bob's Cured Meat Emporium or, as most of the young people call it, jerky junction. Midge, I know how you love jerky. I remember the wonderful turkey jerky we all got for Christmas from you one year. They are going to be a first-time entry into the food court at this year's annual Afton Christmas in July Spectacular. This year's midsummer holiday treat promises to be the best one yet.

We are delighted to welcome the law firm of Bimford, Yardly, Oxnard, and Butternut (BYOB) as this year's presenting sponsors. This is a young company that is all about having a good time, so I think they will be a great fit.

The festival will be held over the four-day weekend during the second week of July. It will kick off with the judging of the holiday lights display. Germaine and Polly Partridge are certainly the ones to beat. Last year they had a tropical theme with decorated palm trees and a tiki bar with Santa as the bartender. This year they have a Mexican theme. Not only is every inch of their house and yard full of colorful lights but they also have a giant piñata hanging from the roof in the shape of a taco salad. Santa and the reindeers are in the front yard and are all wearing sombreros, and Tom's taco stand is set up in the driveway, and one of the weekends they will be serving peppermint margaritas.

The women's club of Afton is sponsoring this year's Miss Summer Yule Log Pageant. I think Cammy Cromwell has a good chance of winning the holiday costume portion. She has made an evening gown from mismatched nativity scenes, and her headpiece is made from two dozen assorted wise men.

To kick off the holiday celebration, the leaders of Camp Chimagowgow are taking all the children to Edna's Encased Meat Museum. One of the major draws is the four preserved bratwursts that were used in the restaurant scene in the final episode of *Two Beers for Eddie* that aired on the Sunshine Network. Also on display are the world's tiniest cocktail wieners and a history of why the hot dog is a ballpark favorite.

The annual Christmas in July parade will feature holiday floats with summer scenes, and many of the marching bands will be playing local island sounds, including the crowd favorite, "Santa Got a Brand New Lei." The grand marshal for this year's parade is Lonzie Karkerplunk, who this year made it seventeen hours in the Afton Dance Marathon and ended up marrying her dance partner, Wally Stinglebrewer. The city of Afton is so darn proud of those two. Their time will be tough to beat next year.

This year's fun-in-the-sun holiday weekend should be a blast. We are looking forward to the annual tree lighting. Don't forget your beach towel.

Zenobia Wrigley

Dear Midge,

Well I've finally done it. I am seeing a therapist. Thanks for reminding me that you had great success with one years ago. It is good to actually have someone to talk to about the crazy thoughts stirring around in my head.

I see Roosevelt Margolis at Licensed Practical Therapy Group. I've tried everything from hypnosis to pressure-point massage but was always too proud to see a therapist.

Although I'm not supposed to discuss the nature of our visits, I'm going to tell you the following things we discussed.

1. Norton Scrambonny cheated me out of three ounces of turkey breast over at Dilly's Deli. That was three ounces I paid for and did not get. I know this because I reweighed the turkey at home. It finally feels good to get that out on the table and process it.

2. I am upset that Oscar and Anna Romancurd allow their dog to widdle in my yard. Small patches of yellowed grass are starting to pop up all over.

3. Becky Bendrover and Alice Arnstramer did not invite me to lady's day at the lodge. They knew how much I look forward to that each year.

And finally,

4. Tookie Larson accidentally sent me a birthday card meant for Delaney Dotson.

I know all of this seems so trivial, but it is certainly issues that mess with a fragile mind like mine. Further, if I let them stew in their own juices too long, I'm liable to explode, and I do not want to put poor Sampson through that. He has suffered with me long enough.

So, Midge, if you're ever feeling troubled or your life is in disarray, you should consult with Roosevelt.

Thinking of you,
Narlene Williamson

Dear Midge,

You are not going to believe this. I went to Garrison's on Thursday to do my weekly grocery shopping and I ran in to Rhoda Fillander. She too was doing her weekly marketing. We shared pleasantries and continued to bump into one another in various aisles.

As I glanced at her down the frozen food row, I noticed out of the corner of my eye that she was loading up on Smith Bros. Frozen Lasagna. I recalled being at her home for dinner last month when she served her famous homemade lasagna, and now I realize that she was passing off frozen as her own. She sure had me fooled.

Sally Diane Rockingham came by for a brief visit and told me about Yarly and Inga Goldsmith winning a trip for two to Yellowstone National Park. The package includes four days and three nights at Rex's Motor Lodge. They plan to leave their dog, Lucky, at the Little Bowwow Palace owned by Orangey Stewart. They leave on Thursday.

I saw Patty Porsman and Quarla Dansberg at the club on Sunday afternoon, and they spoke highly of the luncheon you hosted for the ladies in your Sunday school class. I love when you have themed events. The square dancing with boxed lunches sounds like a good time.

Tina Santa Fe was in Mammie's Mother-2-Be Shop on Thursday. I was picking up a gift for Cathleen Chanworth, who is expecting in November. I got her a couple of nursing bras.

I hope Carter and I will see more of you both this spring. It is such a wonderful time to be alive, and since Gerd's

Greenery has been out to see you, I'm sure your yard looks as good as ever.

Sincerely,
Glenda Glenmeyer

～～～～～～～～～～～～～～～～～～～～～～

Dear Midge,

Selma Snodgrass has agreed to be the chair of the upcoming spring carnival at city hall. Dr. Snodgrass is one of the underwriters of the day's festivities.

This year's theme is Spring into Spring into Fun. I was delighted to hear that Kernie Kantrell and Rander Rollinsworth will serve as leads for the Spaghetti Supper and Hot Dog Eating Contest. Kernie's homemade sauce has them coming from miles away. I think she adds a dash of honey mustard, and that's what sets it apart from all the others.

I am certain that Millicent Montag will try to nudge her sauce in at the last minute. She says it is an old family recipe, but I do believe it is store-bought. I think she adds hot sauce to it because last year Marlon and I were on the toilet for days.

Mavis Moorehead will be serving as chairwoman of this year's silent and live auction. I am sending over a couple of home appliances I won on Name the Song, and Dr. Snodgrass is donating daily teeth cleaning for a year. So basically you would not have to brush your teeth for 365 days. Finally Donald Davishire-Dershon is graciously donating interior design services for two rooms in your home. He and Davin worked miracles in my bonus room.

Midge, you and Reggie should bid on the package. You've been saying for years how much you want to redo your living room. Triple D Design Services are fabulous.

See you on the seventeenth for the carnival.

Muriel

Dear Midge,

Our godchildren Adam and Andrew Anster are visiting for three weeks while their parents go on a second honeymoon. They are basically good kids, but that little Andrew has a mind like no other kid. He is always dressing up in costumes, so we never know what to expect. This week he's been a strange character from *Star Wars*. Next week he'll probably be a ninja, and I'll likely be stabbed with a sword.

Janis Jankersly, our neighbor, has a jungle gym in her backyard. It has not been used in years since her son Bobo got bumped off the swing set by their pet goat. So Adam and Andrew will have free reign to play.

Andrea Berkshire and Catherine Landover were over for tea on Wednesday, and we were discussing the thirty-fifth reunion of our kindergarten class at Mary Michelle Catholic School in South City. Sister Maria is just about the only faculty member left, and we plan to honor her with a lifetime achievement award despite the fact that she used to wash our mouth out with soap and force us to use our nondominant hand in writing class. She's ninety-seven and is still as spunky as ever.

Our reunion will be held at Andre's Banquet Center in Lemay. Since so many in our class have stomach problems and Sister Maria will be there, Andre has chosen a menu of soft foods.

There will also be the King and Queen of the Kindergarten Class of 1973, so that will be fun. I've kept up with some of them, so it will be exciting to see some old faces. I mean I'm certain I'm going to see some really *old* faces.

Midge, got to run. Andrew is on one of Kevin's suits, and I am afraid he's going to trip over the pant legs.

Sincerely,
Wand Wacker

Dear Midge,

We just returned home from visiting our son and his family in Kirkwood. We stayed several days with Paul and Stacy and watched little Craig while Stacy joined Paul on a business trip to Chicago. I had forgotten what it was like being around a little one for more than a couple of hours. Every five minutes, it's either a doodle or spit-up. This one had Steve and I running for days.

I ran in to Kimmel Karlyle at Meow Madness on Saturday. He was getting some new cat food for Lady Marmalade, and I was getting a couple of toys for Janis Jankersly, whose cat just had triplets.

Steve's barber, Tommy Thomas, recently had a cap replaced; so I sent over a plate of deviled eggs while he recuperates.

Darla and Dick Dickenshettz were over for dinner last Friday. They brought Polaroids of their trip to the Great Wall of China. Dick had to have his picture taken every ten feet or so. There were about one hundred pictures of him alone. By the time we looked at all four hundred pictures and then the video set to music, along with a scrapbook, I was ready for them to get the hell out and never come back. But, Midge, Darla has been a lifelong friend, so obviously I could never do that.

Anyway, we're off to see our other grandchildren who live in Creve Coeur. Lee and Lisa are so proud of their little ones, Leita and Darcy.

I look forward to seeing you at the Red Hat meeting soon.

Lady Lonerside

Dear Midge,

We had a lovely time at your home for dinner on Thursday. Your meatloaf was amazing. I must get your recipe and could have kicked myself for leaving your home without it.

Nestor and I were so thrilled to see the addition to your home and the new workout area you put in. Midge, at our age, it is never too early to start working on our extra pounds, although you have had such amazing success with the fat flush and look fantastic.

Robertson and Parker Pansy have asked us to their lake house this weekend. I want to bring them a little something. Not sure if I should take my rhubarb slaw or my tangerine upside-down cake.

I'm sure the men will spend much of their time fishing while us ladies will retreat to the outlet mall for some retail therapy.

Ivy Iverson and Sullivan Stanhope were also invited, but with Ivy's recent procedure to remove moles, I think their participation is up in the air.

I wanted to tell you that I ran in to Gaston Givernest and his wife, Connie Mary, at Wallace Wacker's garage sale on Saturday. They bought a couple of books, two record albums, and some paintbrushes. I found a box of old jewelry and got myself a nifty brooch.

I think Larkin and Sara Love will be having their annual Memorial Day weekend tent sale again this year. I can't wait; you know how I love a bargain.

Got to run; talk to you soon.

Ollie Ragsdale

~~~~~~~~~~~~~~~~~~~~~~~~~~~~~~~~~

Dear Midge,

I'm sorry I have not gotten back to you sooner, but with my recent brush with death, who could blame me.

I was out to dinner with Cindy Lou Cabbage, and on the way in we ran into Frower Forsyth and Barbara Bonworth, whom we asked to join us.

We were over at Vackenshiem's, and I ordered my usual prime rib dinner and salad, when out of the blue I began choking on a cherry tomato and garbanzo bean. How it ended up in my mouth together is still a mystery. You see I do not like any of my food to touch on my plate.

I began to lose my ability to breathe and began turning blue, I am told. In walks Dr. Vastee Vorlick, who began the Heimlich maneuver on me and dislodged the veggies, and all was back to normal.

I had begun to see my life pass before me, Midge, and it wasn't pretty. I realized how ugly I'd been to Yogi, the clerk at Garrison's, and how little I have been tipping Velma at Ursula's Ultimate Updos.

It was scary to say the least.

Finally, I wanted to let you know that your offer for me to play in the mah-jongg tournament was gracious, and I wholeheartedly accept.

Warm wishes for a lovely day,
Edith Enwhistle

Dear Midge,

I ran into Happy Steweyvescent on Thursday afternoon. We were both at the bookstore for a signing by Glenice Watchue. She wrote the marvelous book *Beware of Your Children* about the nonsense that children can pull at any age.

She remarks about how her little ones used to hide in the kitchen cabinets, and when she would open the door, they threw boxes of cereal and other nonperishables at her.

They stared at black TV screens for hours, marched around the room in scary Halloween costumes well after Christmas, and would chug soft drinks and fruit aides when she was not looking, only to be bouncing off the walls within minutes.

She also told a remarkable characterization of her teenage daughters, who would sneak out of the house and get into mischief on their own. One night they both slipped out of their rooms and met up with friends. Later that evening, Glenice got a call from the Arnold Police Department, saying her children were caught smoking behind Fox School.

Beware of Your Children gives parenting tips, including how to monitor your children with surveillance cameras, how to place bars on the windows, and how to lock the kitchen cabinets and put a keyless entry on the fridge.

Midge, it is a quick read and may do you some good with young Simone and Reggie Jr.

The Afton Ladies Book Club will start to read selections from the book next week, and I hope you'll consider joining us.

Further, we plan to read *Gopher Got It* next month, a fascinating book on a gopher that terrorizes a small town.

Shoot, I've got to get going, as Harley will be home soon and expect dinner on the table. Tonight it is beef tips and noodles.

Fondly,
Martina Martinez

Dear Midge,

Thank you for your note. I ran in to Frannie Fuller-Faulkner on Friday while shopping at Garrison's, and she told me of your plans to spearhead this year's neighborhood block party.

I understand from Frannie that this year's party will be an undersea adventure with a genuine aquatic petting zoo. I heard her mention bass, rainbow trout, cod, orange roughy, and salmon. There will also be some crawfish, tadpoles, and a baby shark. That will be some treat.

Frannie told me there would be a cakewalk and a dunking booth. I understand that Mr. Cromwell from the high school will volunteer. Please count me in for my cherry jubilee frosted layer cake.

There will be carnival games and a kid's zone with one of the bouncing ball contraptions. I am excited about the potluck dinner and glad that you've decided to do the meat instead of everybody bringing his or her own. No telling what that could have led to. We would have had a horrible variety of meat pies for sure.

Anyway, Midge, I will see you there. Holler at me if you need any help setting up.

Carlene Chimaque

~~~~~~

Dear Midge,

I heard through the grapevine that you stubbed your toe. I hope all is going well. I bet if you put some ice on it, the swelling will go down, but you have probably figured that out by now.

Karman Kastle Kleerbottom ran over a small child last week with her grocery cart. She caught the back of his foot with the wheels, and he fell down. She then ran over him a second time with her hysteria.

Ellen Earnhardt over at Shea's Sewing Senter had a class on blind stitches, and I was lucky to get in. You know that the blind stitch is tricky, but the eleven of us managed nicely. We also got a preview of the newest Somerset pantsuit patterns for spring. I bought some lime stripe poly-cotton blend and a pattern for a suit with three quarter sleeves. Might be a little garish, but I decided I'm ready for a change.

Peggy Poteete was in the class as well, and she bought some black fabric with a woven silver thread. How bold.

Midge, do you sew? Sewing is great fun, except for those times you accidentally run your finger under the needle.

Looking forward to a visit soon.
Clendenning Willchester

~~~~~~

Dear Midge,

I recently had some car work done at Auto Beauty. Harold Pallermildton and Donnie Davie gave my Chrysler a tune-up. After checking out under the hood, they rotated and balanced the tires. Old Bessie is running better than ever. You were so right; they do a great job.

Dorinda Lipshong and her husband, Lawrence, hosted a few couples from the office at a dinner party last Friday. Brewster is up for a promotion, and we were invited.

It was a lovely affair with cocktails in the living room, followed by a delightful meal of baby back ribs, twice-baked potatoes, and mixed veggies. I swear I think she went to Rib Roundup because the sauce was vaguely familiar. I had only had twice-baked potatoes once before. I cannot begin to imagine why anyone would go to the trouble of baking those suckers twice. Seems like a total waste of time.

She also served collard greens, but I do not eat anything I do not understand, and it seemed like cooked weeds to me. I'm wondering if she did not just pull something from the yard. Brewster seemed to enjoy them.

Midge, her desert was just divine. She made a dump cake. Now I know the name sounds less than appealing, but it was truly wonderful.

You take a can of cherry pie filling and dump it in the pan. Then you pour on top of it a regular cake mix and bake. Nothing else needed.

Good times were had by all.

Bye for now, and we'll talk soon.
Betty Lee Bunderson

~~~~~~

Dear Midge,

It is Coco Catclaw from Olive's Dress Shop in Bella Villa. You came in two weeks ago and special-ordered a dress from one of our manufacturers. Unfortunately the pale yellow double knit with jacket in size 4 is no longer available, but they did have it in a size 2. I'm not certain if that will work.

I wanted to also tell you we got in a new assortment of easy-fit pants. These are the ones with the elastic waist and stay-tight grippers on the inside. We have assorted solids and patterns. Please let me know if I can set a few pairs aside for you.

We have some new ideal-wear shoes with the mega insole for comfort as well as some exciting athletic comfy slides. With your new and improved figure, maybe you would prefer a kicky little platform heel.

Our end-of-the-season clearance sale is now in progress. Huge markdowns on a variety of pantsuits, poly-cotton blend blouses, and spandex muumuus.

Ms. Midge, I certainly hope to see you soon at Olive's, where "Better Bargains from Us Mean Better Bargains on You."

Stay in style,
Coco Catclaw

Dear Midge,

I wanted to let you know that Gus and I took our Buick Skylark over to Sumpter Seagrass at Dale's Deluxe Tire & Auto of Afton. I know you mentioned getting your Pinto over for some work. It was hard to settle on a place to do the work with so many great places to choose from.

Anyway Sumpter pointed out that the auxiliary carbons being emitted from the grind belt on the shaft cylinder are causing ozone issues and that it is also why there was a *kerplunk* when we put the car in reverse.

So we decided to have the grind belt and shaft cylinder replaced as well as an oil change and new tires before our upcoming trip to Eureka Springs.

Yep, we are pulling out on Thursday and plan to drive halfway and stop overnight and see some sights along the way. These include the Southeast Missouri Red Ant Colony, the Caseyville Frontier Park and Taxidermy Museum, and, finally, the Clifftonten Medical Research Laboratory and Gift Shop.

Should be an exciting trip. Thanks for dropping by to get our mail. We'd ask a neighbor, but they are all a little standoffish toward us. See you next week.

Renata Reinmanhopestead

Dear Midge,

Ambrose and I received your lovely anniversary card. Thanks to you and Reggie for the beautiful sentiment. We decided to go to South City to Little Luigi's Midget Pizzeria and Ping-Pong Palace. Ambrose was an all-American in Ping-Pong at Avery State Technical Institute. He would have made the Olympic team too if he had not lost a pinky in a hot tub incident his last year. They kept telling him to keep his fingers away from the jet stream holes, but he can be so stubborn.

Little Luigi's turned out to be a wonderfully romantic and entertaining way to spend our anniversary. Sheena and Darnell Mackleroy told us about it when we were at Eloy Cornwaller's retirement party on the eighth. Little Luigi himself was in the kitchen, along with several other small-stature pizza makers. We stood at the glass windows, watching the pizza being made. It was like magic, really. All we saw was flour and dough rising, intermittently hurling through the air with no visible signs of the little hands doing the tossing.

The food was outstanding. They only offer pizza in one size—small. My guess is the little guys have trouble throwing larger crusts than that. They are known for their unusual pizza pies. The sardine and Spam with white sauce and chives, also known as the Kings Ransom, is a crowd favorite. The Sweetheart Neckline is also a well-liked treat. It has pepperoni, green pepper, olives, and candy corn with a drizzle of molasses.

When they found out it was our anniversary, the little folks sang a special song called "Whatever You Do, Do Not Get Extra Garlic Tonight." It was a touching and romantic ballad. The evening concluded with a heavenly dessert of mint chocolate chip mini pizzas with Provel cheese and a conga line dance to our car.

Midge, you and Reggie need to join us next time.

Here's hoping to see you both soon.
Rosyland Rugstandler

Dear Midge,

I was sorry to hear about the passing of your aunt Pickle. I used to love hearing you regale us of memories down on the farm with summer-time cookouts. Aunt Pickle was always there with her famous bread and butters, her California raisin slaw, and those delightful little come 'n' get its.

I know you will miss her tales of the olden days, when your uncle Art, aunt Silvy, uncle Fizer, and cousins Ansel and Marty were all together at the Madingly family reunions.

Your family picnics also seemed so fun, whereas mine are full of a bunch of hicks from Winchester, and our celebrations drain the life from my little body.

My aunt Sid and uncle Tonka are meddlers and into everyone's business. My cousin Denton and his girlfriend, Paula, always stir up trouble; and Denton's kids, Darla, Dinkins, and Daisy, seem to torture our children.

Aunt Mildred, God rest her soul, was the worst. She screamed because she was hard of hearing, wore her bra on the outside of her housedress, seldom wore both her false plates, and, by the end of the meal, seemed to always be wearing all her lunch. Plus she always smelled of Tabasco sauce. I think she used it as perfume or something.

I envy you, Midge, and send our condolences on the loss of dear Aunt Pickle.

With sympathy,
Dot and Danny

Dear Midge,

Hello, Midge. It is Barker Bobcat form Gerd's Greenery and Landscaping. It is time to renew your contract with Gerd's for weed control. I cannot believe it has been a year already. It is most important to control weeds. You might remember the overgrown yard at Smitty Stackweilers. We tried to get him on board for Weed Whackers' United # 472's seasonal special. But he insisted he could handle it himself.

Well you see how far that got him. The weeds were so tall that the cat got lost. It took him days to mow those weeds down, and they finally found Mr. Genie resting on a thick cluster of tall grass.

A happy ending, yes, and the weeds are finally gone. All of this could have been prevented had Gerds been involved from the get-go.

Mrs. Coldwellstead over on Mulberry Street had a similar situation as the weeds continuously choked her while she retrieved her mail each day.

She called Gerd's when it was almost too late, but we were able to work overtime for a week and get the problem under control, and now Clara's strangulation marks are beginning to go away.

So when all is said and done, I hope this will convince you to sign up again this year.

In appreciation,
Barker Bobcat
Gerd's Inc.

Dear Midge,

I know I promised this letter many weeks ago, but with fall approaching, a cool nip in the air, and all the shenanigans with my family, it seemed impossible; but I finally sat myself down and put pen to paper.

Halloween in my house was a nightmare. The kids changed their minds about costumes a dozen times, and Hugo and I dressed up as well to make it a family affair. This neighborhood really promotes the spirit of community around the holidays, and we had our annual ghosts and goblins parade.

Winnie, our youngest, finally decided to go as a doctor. She has always been very studious. She had a white coat and stethoscope. She looked like the genuine thing. After about ten houses, I noticed a smell and asked her about it, and she pulled open her coat pocket to reveal some sort of concoction. I asked her what is was, and she said it was strawberry jam and a chicken breast. I shockingly said, "What the heck is that for?" and she said, "Mother, it is supposed to be a liver," and she huffed at me. I declare she is sometimes more trouble than she's worth.

Lincoln, our oldest, and his girlfriend got ready at our house. She was wearing tacky makeup and some housewife clothes, and he was wearing nothing but some blue balloons. I hesitated to ask, but curiosity got the better of me. It turns out that they were dressed as a frigid bitch and blue balls. I was stunned and kept my mouth shut, although I was fearful of what the neighbors would say.

I went as a witch and Hugo as a hobo. We did not have to

go to much effort to be in costume, but it was a lot of fun nonetheless.

I saw Mary Pat at the Safeway, and she must have just come from having her hair done. She really should stop going to Shampoo Mary's Afro Doctor because if it gets any worse, she could enter a dog show because of her poodle hair.

We are getting geared up for the fall fest and already coming up with great ideas for the leaves in our yard. I have twenty-five crafts for the Do-It-Yourself Sell-Off and think you are going to love the vests I have made from twigs, fallen leaves, and a glitter stick—they are too cute.

See you Sunday at the tea for Mildred Jobst. It is about time she retired.

Warmly,
Prudence Wilouby

Dear Midge,

It is time for the annual Afton All-Stars Fill Up the Food Bank collection. Your assistance last year and all your homemade jelly bean squares helped greatly. This is my third year to chair this exciting event, and I look forward to working with all of you. Last year was amazing, and our success enabled the Afton Food Bank to distribute food bags to homebound and needy families in the tricounty area. But our work is not done, and I am seeking your support again this year.

Please find attached to this letter a plastic bag to fill up. We are asking various neighborhoods to collect different food groups so we are assured of having all our needs met during the campaign. We will collect these bags the first Tuesday of the month. I am delighted to inform you that your neighborhood will be collecting nonperishable meat products. Truly one of the best categories in my opinion. We suggest canned ham, potted meat, sausages, tuna, sardines, and Spam. These delectable treasures will be needed to serve our growing list of those in need.

Further, we have decided to have two special events to raise both cash and personal-care hygiene products. Cash in the Bank will be held Saturday, September 19, and Fresh as a Daisy will be held the following Saturday. These events will be held in the parking lot of Jerry's A&P. Look for the bright balloons and the tent. We will be serving ice-cold Tab (thanks to Jerry) and home-baked goods compliments of the Afton Ladies' Auxiliary.

We look forward to a great campaign, and your support will get us to the goal of helping twenty-three families this season. Remember, with a full food back, we can fill tummies till they are full.

Thank you from the Afton Food Bank.
Fifi St. Jefferies, Chair

~~~~~~

Dear Midge,

Sylvia and I just got back from Baron County and the Southeast Missouri Bean Fair. Midge, let me tell you this year's fair was better than most. They had the annual bean market, and the navy beans were in spectacular form. I also discovered a new variety of the lima bean.

We strolled around visiting the various booths. Most people were surrounding the kidney bean display, including the amazing works of kidney bean art. There was a lamp with a base and shade made of broken kidney bean pieces and then painted with a decorative wilderness scene.

Capping off the festivities was the crowing of Miss Pinto. Buddy "Pecker" Perkerson served as master of ceremonies, and the Baron County High School tuba ensemble provided music. Cayce Sue Majors was the winner again this year. It's only fair, as she was the only contestant. She looked so beautiful with her crown of genuine diamond chips, pinto beans, and Italian-style green beans.

Midge, we've got to get you and Reggie to the fair next year.

Cordially,
Tandy Tomlinson

Dear Midge,

The Afton Community Players are once again setting their sights on the new calendar year and have decided to present the following productions:

January 8–15: *The Sound of Music,* starring Eric French as Maria. He does have the best voice in a three-county area.

March 1–6: *Paddy McSusan,* a thought-provoking play about a young Irish lad, who is abducted by aliens. This show stars Afton's own Jackson Taylor as Paddy. The Mintz triplets, Mimi, Marla, and Mildred, play the aliens; and Jackson's wife, Starla, is designing costumes.

May 21–27: *The Wedding Reception,* an interactive musical that has the audience participate in a wedding reception, with cake, punch, and Jordan almonds offered each night. The Little Willies will be the reception band, and they will feature classics like the "Chicken Dance."

September 19–20: *Maggie* is an interesting look at addiction in the elderly community. This story takes place as Maggie is getting sober and enters a retirement home. She goes through withdrawal and is adjusting to adult diapers at the same time. With little support from her family, she befriends a gay male nurse and eventually marries the man. This one is sure to get tails wagging.

December 16–21: *An Afton Christmas Carol* is a comical twist on the holiday classic and centers around the lives of some of Afton's most famous residents. Featuring a star-studded cast lead by the incomparable Enis Westbelly and Fanny Figgins. The Studdard Family Singers provide carols at intermission.

As you know, the fireworks factory explosion severely damaged our theater, and we have had to use the employee training room at Basin's Boot Barn. They have been kind enough to erect a stage and allow us to use the staff break room as our backstage / dressing room. We have decided to raise ticket prices by $1.12 to help offset the cost of rebuilding.

The French class at the high school will be providing a French bistro–themed concession stand and offer many treats, including croissants, French toast, french fries, and lettuce wedges with French dressing.

Midge, thank you as always for all you do for the Afton Community Players, and we look forward to having you as our patron again this year.

Kind regards,
Conchita Reynard Robyland
Theater Guild President and Aspiring Actress

Dear Midge,

Today was a great day. We ate lunch at this quaint little place called Deep in the Heart. I had the tuna salad sandwich, and Benny had the patty melt. You had mentioned the delicious sunshine salad, but they were out of maple syrup.

Later we went to the value mart, where we loaded up on toiletries and nonperishable food. We picked up a canned ham, tuna fish, macaroni and cheese, and some cake mixes. I also got some Lady Blue shaving cream and dental floss. Benny got a new CD. Some group named Dixie Darling and the Flatbush Boys. He seems to like them.

Enough about that. Dottie Sanborn was over at Sylvia Mardell's on Thursday, when I stopped by to help set up for the Red Hat Society meeting. Dottie was telling us about her son Snyder, who recently graduated from the Auto Diesel College. He is now manager of Smitty's—a place for your car.

Turns out folks are lining up for Snyder to look under their hood. Especially the ladies in town.

Ralph and Charlene Fulbright bumped into us at Melvin's Matronly Dress Shop. I like to stop in from time to time for a new day dress. Turns out Charlene was attempting to light the stove when one of her dresses caught fire. Luckily the dress was the only casualty, and to cheer her up, Ralph took her shopping.

Stanley sends his regards to Reggie.
Have a great day!
Maude Mettle

Dear Midge,

Jerome Slocomb dropped by to see Ernie on Wednesday morning before work. Luckily I had just put on some coffee and had fresh prune Danish to serve. I stopped by Bradford's Bakery and Alterations. Becky Bradford was there, and we caught up on all the gossip.

She had just taken in a couple of dresses for Inga Herzman, who lost thirty-five pounds from the fat flush after your recommendation. While nibbling on some fresh-baked bread, Inga mentioned that Tamara Townsend just bought a new living room group from Frank's Formerly Owned Furniture. She said it was just lovely.

Marcella Crankshieder and Fern Wisdom just got back from a ladies weekend at Tan Tara Resort in the Ozarks. They said it was the best getaway they'd had in a long time. No husbands, no kids, just two sassy gals out for a weekend of fun.

Finally, Ann Poindexter gave a great talk to the Ladies' Auxiliary about the pros and cons of making your own soup or using canned. Turns out canned is actually a better way to go unless you're strict on taste.

The kids are getting into the snacks, and it's almost dinnertime. More later.

Geneva Gurkstead

Dear Midge,

Well, time flies and spring is already here. We had a lovely Easter, and the children were ever so cute in their Sunday's finest. After church we had an egg hunt in the backyard. Curtis's mother, who is getting more absentminded in recent years, forgot to boil the eggs before she dyed them. Our youngest, Emma Sue, was aggressive in her hunting and stampeded through the yard gathering eggs. Her enthusiasm turned to tears as every egg she plucked from the yard crushed in her hands, and the mess was at times unbearable.

After the mess was cleared, we had a lovely luncheon with both our families. Gene and Milny came in from Tucson, and Ed and Edwina were here with their kids from Calabasas. We had delectable ham and all the trimmings. Lois made her colorful potato salad, and Jeremy and Steve brought a cake decorated like an Easter bonnet. They are a creative bunch.

Our neighbors Khaki and Trevor were also over. I had heard recently a couple ladies mentioned that Khaki was a funeral-viewing hopper. She makes the rounds even if she does not know the departed. She visits with all the mourners and attends many services if she has become particularly close to a group or family. I often wondered how she always stayed so busy. I guess now we know.

I asked her what prompted her to do that, and she said once the children were grown and had gotten lives of their own that she was lonely and thought this was a great way to pass the time. She said she has made so many wonderful friends and has befriended many a widow and now has monthly grief meetings and recipe swapping. They meet the third Tuesday at Graydon's Meat Maze and Taxidermy over in Potter.

I am thinking of attending some viewings myself just to see what all the fuss is about.

Let's catch up soon, dear.

Fondly,
Margo

~~~~~~

Dear Midge,

Turbulent times have struck the McMannus family. I wanted you to be the first to hear before the rest of Afton. I am sad to report that although I have prayed and prayed for our beloved dog, Trumpet, he has finally gone to doggie heaven.

Two Fridays ago, we invited the new neighbors over for a barbecue and a welcome-to-the-neighborhood party. Things were really going great. Mimi and Nora, a same-sex couple, recently moved in to the old Groverland place on the corner. They are the sweetest lesbians, and they adopted a precious little one several years ago, Chin from Korea.

All the kids were playing in the sandbox, and Chin made friends with Trumpet and followed the dog around. Trumpet began to eat some of his food, and that lisp of his got in the way, and one of the hard nuggets slipped from his mouth and bounced off the fridge and hit the child. She screamed bloody murder and needed four stitches on her cheek.

That damn animal control unit locked up Trumpet and ruled that the dog posed a threat to those around him, and we were forced to put poor Trumpet to sleep. The kids have not stopped crying, and we spent $250 for an urn for the dog's ashes. Now I have an urn shaped like a lighthouse, and the kids swear they hear growling while they watch TV.

Needless to say, the lesbians are not speaking to us, and although we offered to cover their medical expenses, we seem to be the targets of a nasty smear campaign. Earlier this week, we found a note in the mailbox stating, "McMannus Family BBQ Turns Deadly—news at ten." I am going to have a nervous breakdown before it is all over, and now we have a dead dog and the kids want a kitten. Midge, that cat better have more than nine lives with this family.

See you soon,
Barbara Ann

~~~~~~

Dear Midge,

We've got great news. Our daughter Barbette got engaged over the weekend. We could not be more thrilled. She is marrying Bauer Brinkman. They have been dating for several weeks now, and we just adore Bauer. He is the son of Bailey and Opal Openmanheim-Brinkman from over in Salem.

She insists it was love at first sight. They met at the Annual Boll Weevil Environment Expo in St. Louis. Boll weevils are a pastime of both these kids.

She is planning an October wedding. It was going to be August, but when I reminded her about how much I sweat, she agreed to move it.

We are heading to scout out wedding gowns this week. She wants one of those really ornate ball gowns with all the bells and whistles, but I recommended something a little simpler on account of her size.

Her friend Kimberly Kastlerock will serve as maid of honor. She is the daughter of Paul and Carol Kastlerock of Oakville. Her other bridesmaids include two cousins from Eau Claire, along with Shelly Shellhorn, Chrissy Conners, Katie Klegler, and Angie Aveldrock.

Bauer has a large family. They are more like a brood, and they have plenty of strapping men to choose from. I am sure he'll use his two brothers, Bailey Jr. and Brock.

Barbette has asked her cousins Dan Dandorff, Jeff Jefferson, and Jake Wornhoser to be ushers.

We are also in the market for some flowers for the wedding

party, the church, and the reception. I think we are going to see Herb Hancock of Hancock's Flowers. They are the best in town.

Her ring is quite stunning, Midge. Bauer bought it at Franklin's Jewelry and Engraving. Fishburn Franklin brought out some lovely settings, we're told.

Finally Monty Richardson and his Karaoke Karnival will provide music.

Looking forward to having you and Reggie as our guests.

Amy and Jason Junker

Dear Midge,

We missed you at the regional auditions for *Super Prize Power Hour.* I swear I think half the town drove up to Kansas City, as I saw so many familiar faces. It was like a cattle call with all of us hurdled in lines stretching out the door at times. We had to fill out lengthy applications and then be interviewed by a series of highly energized casting agents. They must have been on something to be that obnoxious; nobody is that happy to see a bunch of strangers. We all had to practice the show's famous yell by screaming, "Power hour, super power" at the top of our lungs. We yelled it over and over again.

I must tell you, though, I think that compared to all the other contestants, I probably have the best chance. I think they were looking for people with some class, and they could tell I have had some TV exposure in the past. I know it was just a craft demonstration segment on the cable access channel and all, but many see me as a local celebrity. The episode about dried flower note cards was one of the highest rated shows. Vergi Douglas tried to steal some of my thunder, claiming she was also a TV celebrity, but hell, the news reporter only interviewed her because she claimed a spaceship landed in her backyard and killed her rose bushes. I think we all know that that is not how the roses died. If her husband was not such a lousy drunk and got some help with his sleepwalking, he would not be outside urinating on the bushes.

Bernice Jackson looked like a fool in a tangerine-colored polyester jumpsuit. A woman her size should never be allowed out of the house looking like that. To top it all off, she had some rope belt with chimes hanging from it; and when she walked, she sounded like a one-man band. She looked like a parade float. It was just awful.

Lynette and Melvin Snoodle took first prize for the most embarrassing getup that garnered attention. Lynette was dressed up like the *Wheel of Wonder* prize picker, and Melvin was dressed up as Maximilian Morton, the show's host. Melvin could not tame his curly locks, so he looked the part of a clown.

Cornell and Coco Cleveland brought the whole family from Camden, and they had this ridiculous cheer that caused some in the crowd to boo them. All in all it was a terrible chant, and many were not sad to see them eliminated in the first cut.

We will have to wait and see if any of Afton's finest will get selected. I tell you it would be a dream come true to get the chance to be a contestant. Wish me luck.

Judith-Ann Cravers

Dear Midge,

This letter confirms your acceptance and membership to Peel the Pounds weight-loss centers. Peel the Pounds is the new name for the Fat Flush, and I think you will find that your maintenance will be just as effective with our team. As you know, we are an all-inclusive women-only facility that specializes in total weight loss, fitness, and nutritional services.

We have your initial consultation scheduled with Mitzi Morgan for Monday, the fourteenth at 10:00 AM. Be prepared to be here for about three hours, as Mitzi will take measurements, have you meet the staff, get you acclimated to our fitness equipment, place you on a plan designed for you, and help you peel away the pounds.

You will learn a new way to cook and where to purchase our meals, snacks and vitamins, and our specially formulated Fragrant Flush. This is a daily system flush to rid your body of toxins and fat. What is great is that it also cleans your pores and gives you a delightful fresh powder scent that seeps from your declogged skin valves.

Our vitamin regimen will add years to your life, become a key to your successful maintenance, and give you the energy of a teenager just in time to hit our fitness center for one hour per day.

When you graduate, you should see a total weight loss of between three and three hundred pounds on average, and we will give you a $15.35 gift card to Young Guns Forward Fashions and a new hairstyle at Ham's Heavenly Coiffeur. All this along with a certificate of achievement and the weight loss you have longed for. No longer fat and frumpy, you will be the new beauty of your domain.

We look forward to beginning this process and *peeling the pounds* with you.

Sincerely,
Candice Crawford
Program Director

Dear Midge,

I am writing to request an interview with you regarding your recent winning entry in the Greater Midwest Regional Flower Show and Green Thumb Grow Fest. First, *congratulations* on winning Best in Show for your Siamese rose. It is not often that you see two magnificent roses, twins in fact of the same bud. It was truly a stunning sight.

Channel 48 had a crew at the show, and we were able to film some of the judging and the final Best in Show round. We would like to have you as a guest on our news magazine show, *Fabulous Fenton*, and have you tell us a little about your rose growing and your green-thumb abilities. *We* intend to have the first- and second-place winners in several categories, including Most Unusual Plant, Best Nonrose Flower, and Super Flower. We will have callers dial in with questions and will have planting demonstrations with Pandy Larson, owner of Pandy's Petunia Pot.

The show will air live on Friday, the seventeenth, at 11:00 AM, so please arrive about an hour early. One of our production assistants will call you to give you specific details.

Thank you in advance for being part of this special telecast.

Winnie Williams-Waddell
Producer
Fabulous Fenton
WOOF-48 News

Dear Midge,

Kliner Korshead and Francis Forernet had Homer and I over for dinner and a game of Draw the Phrase. Francis served a lovely Mediterranean meal with stuffed grape leaves, a Greek salad, hummus, and baklava. It was truly a culinary delight.

Two members of Homer's twelve-step group stopped by to see him on Friday, Melvin H. and Johnson C. As you know, Homer has not had a desire to play with matches for over three years. Homer was not able to make it to the 7:00 PM meeting because he tripped over an ironing board and broke his knee. He is up walking with crutches and should be back at work in a couple of weeks. I am going to go a little crazy with him at home and may call you to have a girls' day out.

You must get a little tired of Reggie being gone so much. How do you and the kids handle that? I know that they are all in school, but still you all must miss him.

How is Reggie Jr.? I heard from Eugenia Ellwin that he got into some trouble for hanging out behind the school well after campus was closed for the weekend. Nuvell Nightingale told me her son Laramie was also suspended. I know that it was just for a week, but I hope they will not fall too far behind.

Maxine Middlesford mentioned that Simone is now babysitting for Dorinda and Lucinda. I know she is only in the fifth grade, but being held back three times gives her an age advantage.

Finally, Randor Rollins was laid to rest on Tuesday. He was killed Friday in a freak tractor accident. While mowing the lawn, he stood on the seat to grab an apple from a low-hanging tree. He hit his head and fell to his death. As a tribute, his family buried him under that apple tree.

Talk to you soon,
Jarlan Juviet

~~~~~~

Dear Midge,

On Monday I bumped into Unella Cranksley at Joan Annis's forty-fifth birthday luncheon, which was held at the lunch counter at Morgenstern Drugs. There were seventeen of us there, and most of us had the grilled cheese. Joan swears by it, and it was pretty good, I must say.

Thelma Warnerclap and Bronwyn Beggars were there along with Alice Dentribe. It was a lovely afternoon, and it saved me a trip to the mall, as I was able to pick up a few things on my list.

Cornelia Hughlet called to report that she and Adar had a wonderful trip to Cromwell Gardens. All was great until Adar accidentally got some poison ivy. He is suffering all over his body.

Becky Windorff became a grandmother on Friday. Her daughter Noma gave birth to a baby boy. They named him Vinny after his dad. It is hard to believe that Noma is starting a family. First, that terrible accident when she superglued a spoon to her nose. Then those trying times of potty training. You'll remember she was in diapers till she was thirteen. And then there was that experimental lesbian phase, when she dated Sandra Billingsley.

I am glad to see her life has turned around, and she and Vince can have a tremendous go at it.

Can we get together soon for lunch?

Garnet Strathfern

~~~~~~

Dear Midge,

Next Thursday is Bunco at Frieda Formanlang's bungalow on Maple Drive. It is her turn on our rotation, and I'm looking forward to the fun. I am making my turtle soufflé. I use chicken, but it tastes the same.

Betsy Babcock and Arlene Rogers have joined the group, so it will be great to have a couple of extra players.

Paula Renee and Josie Jarvis are joining us again after brief illnesses. Paula Renee sprained her ankle while trying to change an outdoor lightbulb, and Josie broke her toe when one of her flip-flops got wedged between two patio chairs.

On another note, Williamson Williams recently opened Doc's Dairy Bar on Spring Street. He offers whole milk, skim milk, 2 percent milk, soymilk, and chocolate milk all on tap. He has every size bottle imaginable. He offers a variety, including cottage cheese, yogurt, cheddar, and other cheeses (whole, sliced, and shredded). What a wonderful new place to shop.

Amial and Nance Ponestar are hosting a ribbon cutting and reception as they unveil their newly redecorated laundry room. Nance is so excited about it all and has invited fifty family and friends to join them. I am certain you have already received the invitation.

I am not sure what to bring them for a laundry room–warming gift. I'm thinking of some detergent or a bottle of bleach.

See you next Thursday for Bunco and then again on Saturday

afternoon for the party. Don't forget to stop by the Dairy Bar for a half gallon soon.

Warmest thoughts,
Lola Laudenstiper

Dear Midge,

Now that the holidays are upon us, I guess it is time to drag out our old artificial tree. I have saved all the homemade ornaments we've collected over the years. There was a year I was brave enough to try ceramics and then a pinecone-themed year. I also tried sewing one year but really flopped at that one.

I have saved all the construction-paper garland and all cutouts of the children's hands from when they were tots. It is all so nostalgic, but it is also a real pain each year to schlep all this stuff out. The teardown is even harder. Last year I got so lazy that the tree remained up till just before Easter.

We've collected ornaments from the many destinations we've traveled to. We have one from Graceland, Disney World, and from the largest spool of thread in Canyon City, Missouri.

I've got to get busy on my holiday shopping. Merle and the kids are just getting money along with our annual Christmas sweater. This year they are red with snowmen on the front.

The grandchildren are harder to buy for. They each want very specific things. Little John-John wants a board game, Sally Sue wants a doll, and we were asked to get young Malcolm some bed-wetting pads.

I am having my whole family for Christmas Eve dinner. That should be a real treat. Merle is already getting nervous about having all the kids around. Last time they were all here, two pipes from his collection were broken by the time dinner was over.

Midge, wish us well and have a great holiday with your family. Will Reggie be home from the shrimp boat?

Merry Christmas,
Clair Clausman

Dear Midge,

Hope this letter finds you enjoying the beautiful season that has been thrust upon us.

Larnell and Crawford Pigbottom invited Shuster and I to a patio party at their home on Clifton Street. Numerous neighbors and acquaintances were there along with Carlton and Desiree Mintock.

They served smoked pork tenderloin, cheese potatoes, and a garden salad. I brought my delightful three-bean salad, although it almost seems I brought home more than I took. It was not the hit it usually is. I guess that means more for me, as Shuster does not care for my cooking. In fact he outright complains or purposely does not come home till after dinner.

Marjorie and Silas Wintermuster just got back from Mannyville, Illinois, where they toured an aluminum foil factory. They said it was interesting to see how the foil is rolled on the cardboard tubes.

Canton and Missy Rolenmeist told us about the frightening incident involving Canton's brush with death by banana. He began to break out in a severe rash and became fearful of bananas from that day forward. As a joke, Missy bought him a gift card to the Poston Banana Factory Gift Shop, and he started up with the rash when he opened the card.

May Beth Bowkowski entered the Mrs. Afton Pageant this week and plans to compete in earnest despite coming in last place the past five years. She always makes her own evening gowns and usually stumbles on the questions. She also looks terrible in a two-piece bathing suit, and the officials make no provisions for her to wear a one-piece, and I think that is a shame. Her talent portion is always one of the best. This year she will play "Don't Cry for me Argentina" on the harp.

I hope Shuster and I will see you both at this year's pageant.

Hillary Hankston

Dear Midge,

How are you, dear? I had to put pen to paper and fill you in on everything going on with me. There is so, so much to tell.

Austin and I just returned from a whirlwind trip, some pleasure and some not. First we went on our yearly trip to Farmington Falls. We had a wonderful time planned and so much to look forward to. Most of all, just getting away from the hustle and bustle of family and work were what we were most thrilled with. On the first day, Austin and I hiked through the hidden trails carved out along Whispering Wonders State Park. This is such a majestic setting and a great way to kick off the fun. Afterward we enjoyed fruity cocktails on our beautiful terrace overlooking the back parking lot of an industrial park.

On day two, Austin woke up with a severe case of poison oak. So after we were able to get some medication, I took a drive into town and did some window shopping and had lunch. The weather was scrumptious, and it made for a fantastic day. I took to the streets and browsed among the shops on Klinkard Road and did a little shopping. Who could blame me? Austin was not there to stop me. After shopping, I stopped in this divine little cafeteria called The Mess Hall, and after making my way through the line, I took my chipped beef over toast and applesauce and found a seat near a window so that I could enjoy the peace and solitude and a good meal.

No sooner did I sit down than a much older gentleman kindly turned to me and said, "Wonderful weather we're having, ain't it?" I replied, "Yes, it sure is," and went about my business. Not thirty seconds later, he chimed in again that his dog, a dachshund, just had puppies. There were five of them, he said, and one was not perfect. It had a small white dot on its forehead. I nodded and continued eating, thinking he would simply move on. He got up to drop his trash and put up his tray, and I thought this was great, that maybe he will move on. Nope, this time he approached my table and told me that while he was in the service, he had to deliver a baby in midair over the mountains on Wyoming. He got into quite explicit detail, and suddenly, my chipped beef was no longer appetizing. I could not wait to get back to Austin, poison oak and all. I could not imagine what provoked that man to tell me all that he did. Geez! What a day.

When I got back to our room and Austin saw my bags, his eyes got big, but he was so uncomfortable from the poison oak that he could not chide me for my shopping. He then told me that the kids called and said Euvagene, my second cousin once removed, had passed away from a freak roller-skating accident in Florida. Apparently she decided to use her skate key while still in motion. We decided to leave immediately to attend the funeral in Wisconsin. So we loaded up the car and drove nine hours to Manardly, Wisconsin. It was a rushed trip but we had to be there.

We settled in to our room at the motor lodge, and the next day, we drove about twenty minutes to the Bigsby Brothers Mortuary for the viewing. So many family and friends gathered in one place. It was a lovely showing. After saying my hellos to all the people, I meandered through the room, checking out the floral tributes and such. I made a point to notice to plant-to-flower ratio; the odd silk floral spray, which included a stuffed armadillo; and the edible fruit and candy arrangement that someone sent. I mean, please, she can't eat that stuff anymore. I think it was just tacky. I also noticed that several people went in together and sent a balloon bouquet, another strange choice, but this is Wisconsin after all. As the crowd grew more rowdy throughout the evening and family songs and tales were shared, one of the balloons popped and scared everyone to death, except Euvagene, as you can imagine.

The following day after the burial, we headed back to the kids because it was a big weekend with our youngest. Tawanda is graduating from taxidermy school. For her final assignment, she had to stuff and mount a large mouth bass. We ate real well that night.

Midge, it is always good to talk to you. Let's have lunch soon.

Dionne Ditmotherlyson

~~~~~~

Dear Midge,

Our youngest, Timmy, has chicken pox; and the poor dear has broken out in every crook and cranny on his little body. The doctor gave him some medicine, but I've tried a few tricks over and above what Dr. Shoehorn prescribed.

I soaked Timmy in a bathtub of diluted Bloody Mary mix. I tried margarita salt on day two, and I made eighteen large pots of oatmeal and suggested he stew in that for a while. It was the aforementioned oats that proved most helpful. Dr. Shoehorn needs to learn a few of my tricks.

Sally Pat Filmier referred us to Dr. Shoehorn. He treated her son Nathan when he had two dimes stuck up his nose. Several years ago, he treated Noma Windorf, when she superglued that spoon to her nose.

Jeanine Moistener stopped by to bring me a Bundt cake. She learned how emotionally distraught I was at coming in dead last in this past week's league bowl. It is the worst I've done all season. I've got to get out of my slump and improve next week.

Laura Steinerstopper bumped into me at Ham's Heavenly Coiffeur. We were both getting perms. By the way, your new auburn color and that divine style look wonderful. Mine was from Ham, and Laura uses Collette. Ham is so gentle with the wash and rinse. I could pay him to do that all day.

Arlene Clonersled told me that after the success of Garrison's White Sale, they intend to do a Green Sale next week. I plan to stock up on bell peppers, broccoli, cucumber, lime

Jell-O, guacamole, and Easter grass. Looks like it will be another great day of shopping at Garrison's.

Hope to run into you there.

Coriander Johnson

~~~~~~

128

Dear Midge,

Devere and Zilpha Owentrot met Marvin and I over at Clyde's Cattle Call BBQ. I had sweet tea and we all had the pig plate.

Siegfried Weiderloafer took over Marlee's chair at Ham's. I am saddened that Marlee moved to a salon over in Crystal City, but Seigy will do a great job, I'm sure.

Garth Martin and his wife, Sandra, stopped by to tell the story about the large pig that was roaming around their neighborhood last Monday. It apparently got loose from the Oxdale's Farm while they were cleaning the pen.

Cecil and Carla Whitfield's two young sons had never seen a pig before, and when the animal started wandering through their yard, the kids screamed and ducked for cover because they thought it was some sort of monster.

Turns out Mae Oxdale was able to lure the pig into her truck and get him back home. It is a harrowing tale from the pigpen to our little town. But it was fun watching the police and fire departments of Afton trying to catch the bugger.

The covered dish supper at Curtis and Mary Ellen Meany's house was well attended by so many from the neighborhood and lodge. We were so thrilled to see you and Reggie there. I took my baked beans and my wonderful custard dessert. Curtis had horseshoes and Jarts. The kids had so much fun with Frisbee and the bubble machine to keep them out of trouble.

Last year, one of the Olander children ended up taking one of the Meany's bikes and rode it down the street to a neighbor and randomly knocked on a door because he was lost. He needed to use the bathroom and asked for directions back to the party. Poor thing, I think that taught him a lesson.

Well, Midge, I've got to get going. Carlton is expecting pot roast tonight, and I'm not close to being ready.

Darcella Ninetraub

Dear Mrs. Clovis,

My name is Hollis Scranton, and I am the new principal at the Jesse James School. Each year at this juncture, we recruit parents to help out at various events throughout the school year.

I've comprised a list of those events as follows:

1. Sixth-grade pet appreciation parade

2. Junior high wrestling roundup

3. Sixty-Ninth Annual Home Ec Bake-Off

4. Fifth-grade dance recital

5. End-of-the-year book burn

6. Seventh-grade production of *Ben Hur*

7. Vernal Equinox Weenie Roast

8. Eighth-grade field trip to Meremac Caverns

9. Spirit week bonfire

10. Ann Margaret's birthday celebration

As you can see, we have an aggressive display of events this year. We are counting on you to assist us again this year.

Once again, this year we will have our parent registration and kickoff party at Zinger's over on High Street. They have the best chicken fried steak in Missouri according to *The Cluckster Magazine*. The annual ranking of chicken and chickenlike products ranked all restaurants in Missouri.

I personally do not go anywhere without consulting the guide to chicken.

Mrs. Clovis, I personally look forward to meeting you and having you on board our parent team.

I remain sincerely,

Hollis Scranton
Principal
Jesse James School

Dear Midge,

I got a call from Mary Ann Weedenblocker, who is preparing for her son Maximus to wed Ms. Lonna Dawton of Ladue.

One of her responsibilities is the rehearsal dinner. She and Art thought maybe Ragstone's in the strip mall, but I referred them to the Stone Mansion. It is much nicer, and they offer a buffet dinner along with drinks and a dessert bar.

I suggested the chicken breast, green beans with pearl onions, new potatoes, and a garden salad. The iced tea and the pudding pound cake off the bar is a fantastic finish.

Enough about Mary Ann. How are you, Midge? How are Reggie and the kids? I was saddened to hear about Aunt Pickle. She was always a hoot at neighborhood parties.

Collette Darnbottom and Madeline Inkster invited me to a coffee party on the seventeenth, and I would love for you to join me. It is also the fiftieth birthday for Madeline, but she requested no gifts, so I am giving a gift card.

Well it is the end of another season, and I'm looking forward to a change of scenery. Looking forward to seeing more of you as soon as possible.

Till then, Midge,
Kolleen Conway-Lawrence-Shienolt

Dear Midge,

It was lovely to get your call Tuesday last, and I am ashamed at myself for not writing you earlier. I've been busy with preparations for the semiannual corn dog festival. As you know, the corn dog has long been the official food of Afton.

This year the CD committee has decided to make Hilda Primwater chair. You may know Hilda from her jewelry store, Bling 'n' Things. Sometimes Hilda has a clearance table with discounted jewelry. I found a lovely necklace that is missing a few stones, but in passing, it is not even noticeable.

This year, Skip Branstar will dress up in the corn dog mascot costume and lead the parade to the city center. There we'll find corn-dog vendors from many cities with their own version of the corn dog. Last year Barney Whitaker from Graybar had a lovely kielbasa with a blue corn coating. Marlon Masterson from Gurnee also used his imagination and created bite-sized corn dogs using cocktail wieners. Young Debbie Doomer, daughter of Dorcus and Sandra Doomer, is competing for Little Miss Top Dog.

If lasts year's festival is any indication, we're in for a great time.

Midge, see you there along with Reggie and the kids.

Alice Westchesterson

Dear Midge,

I went to a lecture by Carlyle Cross-Collier on Saturday. Her talk was about reaffirming your womanly sensuality. She made some lovely remarks about getting in touch with the real you. I remembered your involvement in ASLUT (American Society of Ladies Unmentionables and Toys), and I thought I would try out a few things from your most recent catalog.

I wanted to get the following:

1.   8491-B   Tickle Me Feather (Red)

2.   7435-1   Dandy D's Leather Whip

3.   1357-2   Edible Panties—Size Large

4.   5812-1   Leather and Lace Starter Kit

I think that will be all for me at this time.

In the interim, Marsha Manchester and I were at Dilly's Deli last week and ran into Toler Barksdale from Mad Myrtle's Meltdown. I am thinking of taking all my old gold jewelry down there and having it melted and made into a new setting for my wedding ring. I've never like the one Wilber gave me and think it's time to use my voice and get a new design.

Anton Meriwether from over in Fenton stopped by to see Wilber on Sunday after church. They are working on the annual french fry feast put on at the local VFW. I've been looking forward to it for the last couple months. Last year's feast proved to be an enjoyable event with french fry entries from seven states.

I so enjoyed the entry from Tennessee. They were sweet potato fries. They were just wonderful, Midge.

I also liked the taste of the fries from Kansas; they were marinated in molasses before cooking. And the entry from Maine was french-fried apples.

So, Midge, we expect to see both of you at the feast.

Quinn Smilee

Dear Midge,

Thank you for your recent call. It was good to hear from you. It sounds like you and your family is in for an exciting season with all the comings and goings of those around you.

I stopped by the Mall of Afton last weekend to pick up a few things. My, has the mall changed so much recently.

I went in to a new dress shop called Hey Lady! and found several items on sale. That is where I ran into Aquanetta Barnham, who was looking for a new church dress.

Next I dashed in to My Where Does the Time Go to get a battery for Arthur's watch.

Then I bumped into Sally Kearny, who followed me in to Read Me, where I could pick up a copy of *Quilters Monthly.*

It was off to Nails by Jasmine for a mani and pedi. She does a great job, and I even bought a toe ring.

Finally I darted through that new store, Gizmo's, where they sell all that crap from TV. Arthur wanted the Dandy Fisherman, and I wanted to get Ester Nutley one of those cookers that make the easy meals with the two compartments. If you ask me, all of it is such a waste of money.

Let's do get together soon for some face-to-face time.

Cordially,
Lorna Langlover

Dear Midge,

Today the lunch bunch and I went to Zany Ziggy's for lunch. They have the best salad bar around. Most of us ate the all-you-can-eat salads while Ester and Beatrice chose the fish tacos, although both had wished they hadn't.

Sorry you could not make it this month, as I understand form Sandy Sanderson that you clipped your toenails too short and that you could not put your feet in to shoes for a week. Hope all is better now.

Delilah Dandy ran into Gauer and Glory Vavershank last Saturday night at bingo. I heard that Glory won big with a coverall. She also plays the scratch-off tickets in the Tristate Lottery and won fifty dollars. She really has all the luck.

Youcee McRae had his deviated septum repaired on Wednesday. We lifted him up in prayer at church.

Irene Scramistoff discovered she has a lazy eye. It is about time. Recognizing the problem is the first step.

Darlene Dooright has finally scheduled surgery to fix her lopsided breasts. I am so glad that nightmare will soon be over.

Finally, Riley Bojangles and Kliner Fitzgerald have announced that after years of trying, they have adopted a beagle puppy. They have named her Sue Ellen.

Midge, do try and make it to the next lunch bunch. They are not the same without you.

Love and Joy,
Ursula

Dear Midge,

Niquila Nedernizer down the street gave me a delicious recipe for deep-fried shortbreads. While I had some trouble getting them, I was finally able to get them from Madge's Meat Market on Simple Street. I ended up with two dozen.

So I fixed them according to the recipe, and Fromer and the kids loved them. It was not until Fromer mentioned my delicious meal to Hankins Hadelberry that things took a turn for the worse. Hankins told Fromer that shortbreads were actually castrated bull testicles. When I found this out, my stomach turned. The sad thing is they were really good.

Fromer went to his monthly Plumbers Association meeting on Monday night. He ran into Reggie's friends Vinings Randall, Winthrop Doherty, and Tobias Tethering. They mentioned that Reggie had a successful run recently while out on the boats.

Russ Thornbuster gave a remarkable presentation on the correct usage of the toilet snake, a device used to overcome nasty blockages deep within your toilet.

Oscar Orland and his wife, Carmen, visited us last weekend from their home in Sullivan. We took them on an architectural tour of St. Louis and then on to Milo's Pretzels for a tasty treat, followed by Lupe's Frozen Custard.

We had visited them several months ago, but there really is nothing to do except visit the dollar gallery and the Crystal City water bottle factory. Let me just say that is not too much fun.

Midge, I was going to send you the recipe until I got the unfortunate news. Let me look for a better one.

Until then,
Prentice Ponderly

~~~~~~

~~~~~~

Dear Midge,

I just had to write and tell you what I overheard today at the market. I was standing about three feet away from Sissy McGovern at the deli counter at the A&P as I was ordering a pound of boiled ham and Sissy was getting olive loaf. Anyway, Patty O'Connor came in and you could tell she did not want to see anybody she knew. She had on no makeup, and her hair was in rollers, and she had on a rain bonnet. The poor dear was a sight. Sissy spotted her, of course, and that is when I overheard the juiciest story.

Apparently Patty has a brother over in Arnold, and he has been living with a woman for some years who has recently gotten quite sick. Patty's brother Buford has always been on the sickly side anyway, and since he is a self-employed taxidermist, he pays his own medical expenses, and now with a girlfriend in such bad shape, he has to take on some of her health-related expenses as well. As it turns out, the girlfriend has a sister in the military who is a lesbian and has been in a relationship for fifteen years with the same woman. Well now the lesbian sister of the girlfriend is going to marry Buford so that he can be enrolled on her insurance. And to top it all off, the partner is going to be maid of honor. I about fell out in the store because this is a tale of such deceit. Lordy, Midge, this is an all-out scandal, and I heard about it first. It is so exciting, and I hope I get an invitation so I can see how all this will play out.

Don't get me wrong; I support the gays. I mean for crying out loud, Ham has been doing my hair for years, and I would trust him with my children. So all I can say is more power to them. Maybe we should throw them a wedding shower.

Let me know your thoughts.

Janey

~~~~~~~~~~~~~~~~~~~~~~~~~~~~~~~~~~~~

Dear Midge,

I was at the greeting card store the other day, picking up a card for Helen Protoski (she is recovering from a slip disk she incurred while trying to push the car several weeks ago when she ran out of gas). I was wandering through the aisles, reading the various cards, most of them saying kind words about a daughter, son, aunt, or uncle. These were the kindest, most sincere words, and it got me thinking … how unfortunate that I do not have one of those families. My good-for-nothing brood just keeps getting worse.

As you know, I had most of my family and Stu's family here to celebrate our twenty-fifth wedding anniversary. *What a mistake.* First off, my piece-of-crap husband wanted to know why I was making such a fuss. When I explained that we were embarking on a milestone in our marriage and it was a great chance to celebrate, he said, "Oh yeah, that." My mom was here with Aunt Clara and Uncle Purvis. They drove the new family wagon and had it loaded down with Mom's famous potato salad and some homemade treats. What I did not know is that they stopped in Columbia for a night to pick up my cousin Rose and her son Mil, and they left the salad out in the car overnight. So there was an odor that no spray could get rid of and no usable potato salad.

Our youngest, Carl, was asked to inflate the air mattress so that Clara and Purvis could take his room and he would be able to sleep in the bonus room on the floor. You would have thought I was asking him to cut off his arm. Marsha stayed with a friend, and that gave Mom a room to stay in. Stu's parents and some of his relations stayed at Blake's Motor Lodge on I-57. *Thank God.* On Sunday, all the others arrived, and it looked like a nice day was actually going to happen. That is until Penny and her new baby arrived.

We all knew that Penny had been in a relationship and that just after the baby was born the father skipped town. What we did not know is that the daddy was African American, so we have a beautiful caramel-colored baby in the family. My kids decided to each invite a friend. Marsha brought a nice young man she has been going steady with, and Carl brought his friend Chas. Interesting fellow and a little on the feminine side and wore a pink shirt. But he and Carl are best friends, and I never judge anybody.

Stu was the grill master, and his dad and the uncles gathered to offer their own advice on the perfect burger. Most of the ladies sat in the shade, and my mother could not stop talking about the baby. Enough already.

Dinner was good, and then afterward, we regaled with stories about the old times, family past and present, and each other's aches and pains. Good Lord, it was a contest to see who was taking the most medications or who had the most surgeries.

We received a lovely money tree as a gift from the collected group. I think we are going to get linoleum in the kitchen. Marsha griped what we were not using the money to get something the whole family could enjoy, and I asked if she was not planning to ever be in the kitchen again. She can be quite hateful. She is such the boss witch.

All in all, it was a nice day, but now I need a cocktail, so I must go.

Carmella

Midge Dear,

I just returned from lunch with the girls. You are missed, and I certainly hope that your gout flare-up is quick to depart. Follow your own advice and get in quickly to see Dr. Dillard Dandridge before things get worse. We had just three this week besides me. Cat Conley, Marcie Monroe, and Peggy Pohanka. After a brief period of who's done what and family and health updates, we enjoyed the buffet at The Cluckster on Gravois. I never get tired of the fried chicken despite the twenty-minute wait for fresh chicken.

Cat and Stan just returned from a mission trip to Spokane with their church, and Marcie and Dave are getting ready to go to the Fall Creek Caverns in the Ozarks with a few friends from Dave's job at Walter's World of Brakes.

Peggy was telling all of us the terrible troubles she has been going through of late. Her youngest, Edsel, was kicked out of the Wonder Scouts for cheating on his entry on the man-made car races. He apparently had read that he could weigh down the front of the car to allow it to gain speed down the ramp. He weighted it down so much that it careened over the other cars, causing an eight-car pileup and damaging several other scouts' cars. She describes all this in a way that clearly shows her embarrassment.

Her daughter Shilo also has had some moments recently. Turns out she entered the home ec class bake-off using a published recipe rather than an original one. When she won the bake-off and then subsequently had her title stripped, she faced scorn from the other students and a failing grade for the semester.

Finally Peggy recently used a generic brand of tooth-whitening solution and not only bleached her teeth but also her gums by using too much solution. Now when she smiles, you can see her mouth from space because there is so much glare.

After all the good news, we decided to splurge and hit the dessert bar at The Cluckster. Boy, Midge, did the four of us do some sweet damage there. They really do have some of the best lemon chiffon pie anywhere. I had three slices and felt I needed to be rolled out of the building.

We hope to have you join us next month. We have decided to try Spatts Spam-O-Rama in Bolton, where they have twenty different dishes with Spam.

More soon,

Corrine

Dear Midge,

I just got off the phone with Loretta Linghauser. She had the exterminators at her place all morning. It turns out that, suddenly and without warning, they have been overrun with dust mites. She first noticed them on Tuesday, and by yesterday, they were everywhere. She was forced to call Rodney Rothman, who is the bug guy from over in Tatum. She and Lester are going to have to spend the night away while the whole house is treated.

Loretta has been on the phone all afternoon, trying to get a room for the night. She finally found something in Afton's Chinatown area. She had a connection through Ling Ling Chang, whose husband, Moo Goo Guy Sam, is mayor of Chinatown. They are staying in a deluxe room at The Chow Mien Palace and Oyster Bar. I hear their turndown service is spectacular. They make their own mint-flavored fortune cookies that are placed on the pillows.

On another note, I was delighted to hear that Naomi Nixon and Pedro Jackson are appearing in concert at the VFW on Route 12. This year they are presenting a Captain & Tennille tribute band and are calling themselves Chenille. I think this is going to be one of the best concerts this year. As you recall, they played a concert last year and did a Sonny & Cher tribute concert and called themselves Scare. A good time was had by all.

I sense there is going to be a little "Muskrat Love" going on in Afton that night. Hope to see you there.

Fondly,
Kathy Kay Konrad

Dear Midge,

I hope this letter finds you doing well. On Thursday I was over at Bits and Pieces, picking up some carpet remnants, when I ran into Lilith Snodgrass. She had pep in her step and was positively glowing. She cornered me as I was rummaging through a bin of shag samples, and she began a very passionate conversation about ice cream. I was bewildered at first and could not figure out her dramatic and sudden fascination with ice cream.

She mentioned she was attending a recent ice-cream social and discovered a new flavor that had brought her much pleasure. She talked about trying out various sundae toppings, had tried it in a milk shakes and other frosty treats, continually referring to her new and delightful rendezvous with ice cream. I was shocked when she said she indulges in ice cream three to four times per week. I like ice cream as much as the other gal, but if I had sweets that often, my double knits would no longer fit. I finally moved to the indoor-outdoor carpet display, and she bid me a fond farewell and went on with her shopping.

Later that evening, I was attending the Jesse James School's science fair, where Manny Shoemaker and Thaddeus Warlock won top prize for successfully breeding North Atlantic slugs. A very difficult feat under normal circumstances, but they achieved their success in our harsh Midwestern winter. While I was mingling, I ran into Varnell Paulson, and I mentioned that Lilith talked to me about ice cream for what seemed like hours, and I was blown away by what Varnell told me.

It appears that Lilith has been stepping out on her husband, Oscar, and has been having an affair with some guy over in

Edison. Varnell says that ice cream is code for the romance so that nobody finds out. It was a jaw-dropping announcement about dear friends, whose marriage I thought was rock solid. It got me thinking about all of the strange conversations I have had in recent months and wonder if any of those conversations contained code words.

I guess I envy Lilith a bit. Night after night, she is enjoying ice cream while I am stuck at home with yogurt. Some things never change.

Talk to you soon.
LaWanda Simpson

Dear Midge,

Before I go any further, I wanted to remind you that the Nifty Fifty and Over Synchronized Swimming Team will kick off our season practice Tuesday afternoon, the tenth, at 3:30 PM at the Maynard H. Mehlville Yacht and Aquatic Club. We are looking forward to having you on our team again this year and doubly excited to have Antwon Maxwell as our choreographer. He choreographed the Hazlehurst Housewives to victory last year with his Majestic Mothers Ballet. It was positively stunning.

Last night was the monthly neighborhood association meeting, and our chairperson, Brunilda Barnhill, got right down to business, as we had a serious topic to discuss. It seems that earlier this month, there was a home invasion at the two-story house of Griselda and Graham Gotlieb. They were held at gunpoint by two masked thieves, and after fifteen minutes of sheer terror, the thieves made off with six cans of tuna and a boxed cake mix. I just sat there in disbelief, listening to the horror, and the only thing I could think of was that I could not believe that Griselda uses boxed cake mix.

In other news, they announced the new officers for the upcoming year for our neighborhood association. Hortensia Hagewood is the new president, Alfredia Morganford is the secretary/treasurer, and sergeant at arms is Tyler Thompson. They are a ruckus bunch, and I think our monthly meetings are about to get a bit livelier.

I need to run. Rutherford is grilling pork steaks tonight, and I have to watch his every move. Last time he did this, he left them on too long, and we ended up with bacon.

Cheers to you and yours,
Clotilde Coxly-Cawthon

~~~~~~~~~~~~~~~~~~~~~~~~~~~~~~~~

~~~~~~

Dear Midge,

Cordovia Smythe and I just got back from a wonderful Star Shine Weekend in Wichita, and we missed you this trip. As you may recall, I am past president of the Afton Star Shiners and Cordovia is in the midst of a fierce campaign for vice-matron. She is up against Bettina Bordeaux, who has spent tens and twenties of her own money in nasty smear tactics to discredit Cordovia. However, it actually looks like it may have backfired on Bettina, as many of our sisterhood have backed off their support of her as the campaign nears its climax.

The Star Shine Weekend kicked off with a parade of nations and the singing of our national song of sisterly glory. Each time I hear "Embrace Me, Sister Girl" I am overcome with emotion.

After the opening session, we broke out into the various leadership awareness groups we had registered for. My first group was Passionate Presentation Skills. We went around the room and introduced ourselves after our Star Shine leader demonstrated a new introduction technique. I was nervous to say the least, as I am not a good public speaker, and thus is the reasoning behind wanting to learn to be a more confident communicator.

The leader said, "Introduce yourself and say some positive and interesting facts about yourself as a way to break free of the bondage of the fear of public speaking." After several sisters took part, it suddenly became my turn. A hush fell over the crowd, and I began, "My name is Katydid Tidyman, and I enjoy cod liver oil twice a day, collecting placemats, cleaning up after my incontinent dog, and I am proud to be the reigning Naugahyde tanning champion of Greater Afton."

My fellow sisters were wide-eyed and drop-jawed. No one said anything, and we quickly moved on to the next lady. From that moment on, I felt a renewed sense of confidence and surer of my destiny than ever before. As the Star Shine Weekend continued the following day, I could not help but notice many of the ladies pointing at me and whispering amongst themselves. A sheer moment of pride came over me until I realized that I had put my girdle on over my pants.

I hope I have better luck next year.

Fondly,
Katydid Tidyman

Dear Midge,

Harvey and I are getting ready for our trip to sunny and tropical Lithuania. We are going to a little-known city on the southern tip called Witzelbergerton. In preparation, I went to Forever Tan: Where Black is Beautiful. I bought the bronzed bombshell package that guarantees cocoa complexion in just thirty-six visits. I am going every half hour to get ready for our departure on Saturday. I cannot wait to fill you in, Midge.

We are arriving in Witzelbergerton on the final day of Erock D'Zuna or the Turnip Festival. All the villagers celebrate everything turnip, and on the final day of the monthlong festival, there is a big parade; a concert featuring Dottie Claudette, Lithuania's most popular country music star; and fireworks after the crowning of the Turnip Queen, whose sole responsibility throughout her yearlong reign is to add a secret ingredient to the 104-year-old turnip stew recipe.

Last year's queen, Bambi Shanita Balzekas, added cream of tartar. Nobody ever eats the stew because the stench is so overpowering, but it is an age-old tradition.

In order to fit in with the locals, I ordered a specially designed Kontusz for the parade. Much to my surprise, I discovered it is only worn by Lithuanian male nobility, and I would not be permitted in to the country if I wore one, so I am just going to wear my old standby patchwork quilted skirt and matching vest. I think I should be okay with that.

I never imagined we would go on such a wonderful trip, but after years of saving green stamps, I decided to cash them all in. I had 417,352 green stamps. It was enough to pay for one of us to go, and Harvey decided we could dip into our savings so I could go with him.

We are so excited and I will be sure to send a postcard.

See you in two weeks,
Elwanda Kimber

Dear Midge,

Before I get to the good stuff, I wanted to tell you that Delphia Dorlottstinger broke her proximal interphalangeal joint last Thursday while trying to remove shelf liner from her kitchen cabinets. The broken knuckle will take about six weeks to heal.

Well, Midge, now that we have reached the end of September, it is time to look forward to the Thirty-third Annual St. Juanita of Peavely Picked Egg Boil and Fall Festival. Every year all of Afton is twitching with excitement, and every house in town are getting their eggs ready.

Among the highlights of this year's three-day festival is Tawny Tellweird, who will read from and sign copies of her new book, *The Devil Made Me Do It: A Beginner's Guide to Expert Deviled Eggs.* The exciting kids corner is back and will include many games and crafts and the egg on a spoon race that is always a big hit. This year the organizers have decided to spice things up by having racers balance egg-drop soup on their spoon and race to finish line.

After the fluffy meringue cook-off, the festival will conclude with a dance on Main Street. This year for the first time, we will have the sizzling Latin sounds of Eggsalante. They are going to be promoting and performing selections from their number one cassette, *I'm All Yolked Up.* Some of the hits include "Shell-Shocked," "Shattered," "Over Easy," and their biggest hit, "I Knew It Was Love the First Time We Poached."

The Ladies' Auxiliary is working hard planning for this year's Sunny-Side Up Café. They will serve up a luscious array of egg salad sandwiches, fried eggs, omelets, quiche, and scrambled eggs. They will also have a wide variety of flavored and spiked eggnogs.

The grand marshals of this year's chicken coop parade are Royce and Virgie Cloydstramm, who are the owners of the Midwest's largest egg-laying farm in Festus. They will be riding on a float sponsored by Garrison's Groce-rama, who will feature Cloydstramm eggs exclusively, which is big news for Afton. The float is going to feature a super-sized carton of eggs and Royce and Virgie dressed up as giant hens. The children's choir at St. Juanita's will be on the float, throwing out marshmallow eggs to all those on the parade route.

Sandria Yardlesburg, the reigning Clucker Queen, and her court will ride behind in a giant chicken crate made especially for the parade. Her reign comes to an end at the finale of the festival, and Britta Bromwald, who was elected by secret ballot by a panel of specially selected egg aficionados, including Felicia Frockingharny, Esperanza Gomez, and Octavia Rimshutz-Burgerman takes over as queen. I also understand that there might be an egg hatching in Britta's future. If she is not able to fulfill her reign, the second runner-up will take over, and this year that was Scotty Marshalingle. Should be interesting.

See you at Boil,
Georgiana Ginderstaldt

~~~~~~

Dear Midge,

Orlando and I just got back on Thursday from our church trip to Branson. We had a wonderful time, and the highlight of our trip was getting to see the dance troupe Vegetation. They are an amazing environmentally green group, whose costumes and stage design are made from things you would find in your garden.

There were interesting head pieces made from endive and cabbage and one sensational outfit constructed entirely out of spinach. All were inspired creations and gave me wonderful ideas for Halloween.

On Saturday night, we had dinner at Irving Warfell's Gravy Boat in Ballwyn. Melvin and Herlinda Genovese joined us. The service was extraordinary, but the menu seemed a bit limited. We each had three near beers, four picked eggs, and half-a-dozen fish sticks. To top it off, they were out of tartar sauce and only had maple syrup.

We stayed for the live music. Saturday night featured a musical treat from Here Kitty Kitty. They are a folk group who performs songs with feline references. They did several of their crowd favorites, including "My Love For You Has Nine Lives," "You're Purr-Fection," and "Crazy for Catnip" or, as the crowd calls it, "The Feeling Frisky Song."

We are going to Mozelle Monserrate's wedding next weekend at St. Archibald's Church and look forward to seeing you and Reggie there.

Much love,
Donna Dee Drummand

Dear Midge,

So much to tell you. It feels like I have not seen you in forever, but know that a week or two seems like a lifetime for the two of us. On Thursday I took the kids to Stuff 'n' Things for some back-to-school supplies. They all got new backpacks and then left the rest up to me. I remember like it was yesterday when I got to go BTS shopping. Everything I needed for my pencil box along with loose-leaf paper and a new three-ring binder. I was in hog heaven. Those were the days. Now each school provides a list, and suddenly after twenty damn minutes, I am out two hundred bucks. Such is life.

Carmine and I visited Germantown last weekend. I so wish you and Reggie could have joined us, but I know your condition flared up, and that prevented you from traveling. I hope that your Panthrax, or more commonly called Dish Pan Hands, clears up in the near future and you can join our next adventure.

While we were in Germantown, we visited Harry's Haus of Schnitzel and tasted some wonderful treats. We also test-drove some of the newest offerings from Astrid's Autostadt, including some of the new smart cars. Carmine decided this was much like driving a go-kart. He had too many pastries and a difficult time getting out of the car. He will never learn. Later in the day, we toured a German brew house, and Carmine and our friend Nestor got a little tipsy. Our tour guides for the day, Luca and Lena Schmidt, pointed out all the history as we took a driving tour of the old town.

We saw the pet shop where the German shepherd is the popular pet these days. We saw the Bauer sauerkraut factory, which is the largest outside Bavaria. We toured the famous wax museum with distinctive wax statues of some famous Germans, including Wolfgang Weiner, the inventor of the hot dog; Brigitte Schmid, the inventor of German potato salad; Angelika Kraus, the world-famous author of *Damn, There Goes Another Dachshund*; and, finally, Dieter Douglas, the famous German talk-show host and half brother to American icon Sven Svenheider, the fashion designer to the stars. He is the wiz kid who designed the vinyl romper that Victorina Middlesex wore to the premiere of her documentary, *Mad Sow: The Adventures of Pig Boy.*

Our day ended with a lovely dinner at Germantown's Sausage Sanctuary, where we dined on a buffet of traditional German delicacies, including goulash and rabbit ears. It was Oktoberfest, and we enjoyed dancing and merriment to the wee hours of the morning. I cannot wait to go back next year.

See you soon, dear.
Edna Rae

Dear Midge,

HAPPY HOLIDAYS! I cannot believe the festive season is upon us. I hope I will see you at Nellie Novinger's annual eggnog extravaganza. She always knows just how to kick off the yuletide in style. I thought last year's party was just delightful, especially with the anatomically correct gingerbread men. I hope she knows that will be hard to top, but I have no doubt she will do it.

I ran into Babs Bingham last week at Murph's Midtown Mall. She was doing a little early shopping at Finkman's Department Store. I turned the corner, and there she was in the arms of another man. I could hardly believe my eyes. As I leaned in to get a closer look, I was relieved to see that it was only a mannequin that she had knocked over trying to fight for the last Santa hat trimmed in genuine rabbit fur.

I just got back from a rehearsal for the Christmas pageant over at St. Ruby's. This year's program promises to be the best ever. Many of the great performers from Afton will be part of this holiday tradition. Kippy Kasper and Helene Hoffman will perform classic Christmas songs, such as "Conway the Cowboy Santa," "Lord That's a Big Ole Tree," and "Don't Go Crazy, It's Just Snow."

Keifer Koons and his band, The Ex-husbands, is the house band and Patty Pickler, the organist at the church, will also play a special role. The church choir has put together a musical salute to Christmas around the world. They will sing "It's a Wurst Christmas" from Germany, "There's a Wonton in My Stocking" from Japan, and everybody's favorite, "It's The Season for Salsa" from Mexico. This year's program will be bilingual, featuring both English and British translations where needed.

The adult art classes at Ziegler's Craft World will display the Nativity scene made from toothpicks, old matchbooks, and twist ties. They have even used silly putty and modeling chocolate to mold the characters in the manger. The baby Jesus is made from a cocktail wiener with a gumball head.

The students at Miss Darla's House of Dance will be doing the dance of the frisky fairies, and little Nona Narvel will do a solo to the song "What a Great Gift, but I Already Have One Of These" by Lionel Ruggio. She is already shining up her tap shoes.

Finally Marvin Masters will showcase his many birdcalls by doing his own rendition of *"Hark, Who's That Harold?"*

I look forward to seeing you and your family throughout the holiday season. Don't forget to get your copy of the *Candy Cane Press* from Loralee Langston. This issue has her recipe for fruitcake gumbo.

Cheers,
Rosilyn Raffly

Dear Midge,

Just a note of thanks for the wonderful potted meat casserole, glazed celery salad, and hot cross buns you sent over last week. It was a lovely treat. You are always so thoughtful.

Last Saturday I attended the bridal shower for Francine Figglestien thrown by Marva Monroe and Audrey Longo. The ladies had a fantastic spread of food from Eager Beavers Catering. The cake was especially tasty with the ginger, cherry, and chestnut filling.

Francine received so many beautiful gifts. She got a Fry Wizard, a Filbert Smoker, A complete set of Lock-Tite plastic containers, including the highly sought-after salad separator, and a Collier Carrot Caddy. As a surprise, her cousin Bulah gave her a framed copy of the secret family recipe for sugar-cured sardines.

Her mother, Marjorie, gave her a stunning hand-embroidered handkerchief with a two-leaf clover on it. It was handed down from her grandmother, who never completed the other two leaves after she ran out of thread. It will be a prized possession for sure.

Finally, next week marks the centennial celebration honoring the historic Battle of Afton. There will be a parade down Main Street featuring The Salem Serenaders, The Drum and Bugle Core of Arnold, and Art Millnard and the All-Tuba Marching Band, featuring solos by Farley Forrester and Jasmine Jenkins. I hear the grand marshal of this year's parade is none other than Trixie Snodgrass, recently crowned Corn Dog Festival Queen.

After the parade there will be a turkey jerky cook-off,

butterscotch pie tossing, a poetry reading by Sherman Stanhope, whose poem "I Think I'll Learn to Smudge" won the Mount Kooner literary award last year. The evening will be capped off with dancing under the stars to the musical stylings of Willard Warble and the Trench Coats.

Looking forward to seeing you there.
Betty Mary Sipster

Dear Midge,

I could hardly wait to write you and give you the details of the upcoming Independence Day celebration. I am happy to report that Afton will once again play host to the tricounty festivities. This year's theme has been a tightly held secret, but Mitzi Maytag, this year's cochair, made the announcement this morning at the League of Merry Windows Breakfast held at Carlson's Cornbread Café.

Mitzi revealed that America: The Perfect Place to Be a Vegetarian would be this year's theme. Last year we went with the canned meat theme, so this year it was unanimous that we go in another direction.

Lulu Lancaster, the president of the Afton Town Council, is making it her mission to have a very diverse celebration this year. We have narrowed down the list of participants, and I am delighted to tell you that The Claxton Cloggers will debut a new number, and thanks to new costumes donated by Billy Barley from Barley, Biggs, and Bigger, they are sure to turn a lot of heads. The new costumes consist of red tube tops and blue skorts, along with white leg warmers. We had a potential disaster in the making, Maude Masters, who has unusually large calves, could not fit into the leg warmers; so at the eleventh hour, team captain Farrah Funke pulled out a couple of sweater vests and some ribbon, and now Maude looks just like the other cloggers.

Additionally, Sippy Slatstone will sing her original song "I Don't Mind Being Patriotic, But Red Is Not My Color." She will be accompanied by the Afton Banjo Brigade.

The Tilpot Trio will also perform some of their greatest

hits. Some of their crowd favorites include "My Lima Bean Serenade," "Can I Get Fries with That," and their former number-one single, "She Used to Be a Tart."

Members of the Afton Community Players will perform selected scenes from the upcoming musical *The Toilet Paper Diaries* featuring Yolonda Grassman and Carl Carlyle.

The Ladies' Auxiliary will hold the annual Star Spangled-Food Fair with entries from all over the region. This year the entry to beat will be Nini Nimble's Yankee-Doodle Noodle Casserole.

I think one of the highlights will be the traditional recitation of the names of the former presidents of the United States and their birth dates. I mean, really, does it get any more patriotic than that.

We look forward to seeing you and your family on July fourth. Bring your sparklers.

Molly Moody Masterson

Dear Midge,

I just returned home from the visitation and viewing for Loretta Primlegger. She was a mentor to all and will be missed by the Ladies' Auxiliary and the Council of Afton Arbor Day Planters. Who knew a fever blister could go so wrong so quick? I just saw her last Monday. There was a wonderful showing over at Coots & Smyth Mortuary. Dexter Primlegger and the children did a good job with the arrangements. Loretta would be proud. She was presented in a copper-and-black trimmed casket with rhinestones and emblazoned with her monogram, LIMP (Loretta Inez Mildred Primlegger). It was lovely. She was laid out in her teal suit with the little inchworms all over it. They were her favorite. I thought it was strange that they had her fanny pack on her too. Sorry you missed it and hope the trip to Lusterville Caves was enjoyable despite all the rain.

There were wonderful old pictures of Loretta with her family and many friends. There were flowers everywhere, even a cactus. Somebody really knew her taste. The children and grandkids put some special mementos in the casket. A picture of her beloved dog, Snittle; a little statue of St. Norbert; some pictures the little ones drew of Nanna; and, oddly, a package of jelly beans, potted meat, some saltines, and a can of Tab. Little Dexter III did not want Grandma to get hungry, he said. I thought that was precious.

Some of Loretta's cousins and their families came over from Samson City. Country cousins to say the least. Two of the girls were in cutoff shorts. Loretta's cousin Beaufort was in overalls and a T-shirt with a tie, and his wife, Laddy Mae, was in a black dress more suitable for working the street corner.

They brought a tray of chocolate sandwich cookies dipped in guacamole and a bouquet of flowers they obviously picked up at the market and handed them to Dexter wrapped in a paper towel dripping with water.

Earl Mooncan wore his nametag from his job at the hospital even though he had on a suit for the occasion. Needa Norbit shared stories of when Loretta was Afton Sausage Queen in '73, and again in '74, when Cissy Crawford was disqualified for bribing the judges with her imitation crabmeat chowder. Hell, she should have used the real stuff, and then maybe she would have won.

The chorale from the Little Arborettes sang several lovely songs in tribute to Loretta and then the entire parlor sang Loretta's favorite song in three-part harmony. It was a beautiful rendition of "That Old Slipper Hurts My Foot." Not a dry eye in the place.

Several of the ladies asked me to join them for a drink and raise our glass to LIMP. We went to the Bird House, where it was happy hour, and they had half-price Cornish game wings.

See you soon, my dear Midge,
Dovie McDoogal

Dear Midge,

Baxter and I just got back from our annual pilgrimage to the Country Music Festival in Copenhagen, Denmark. This was our sixteenth year, and we always have such a good time. This year's festival included some old favorites. The Sugar Cane Kids sang many of their hits, including *"Cow-Tippin' Promenade."* Didi Daniels and the Wolf Pack sang their recent hit, "I Just Got Over Him and Now I Want Him Back but He's Got a New Tramp."

This year some up-and-comers from the highly successful Denmark country music scene made appearances at the festival. Gustav Gundersnap and Frida Hansen sang a beautiful duet of the country classic "Teenie Tiny Twanger." We also liked Anders and Astrid's version of "Scandinavia Rodeo."

While we were over in Denmark, we did some sightseeing. We have always enjoyed the local culture, and this year was without exception. We toured the Jorgensen Index Card Factory. We were especially fascinated with the fact that they still hand draw all the lines on each card. Definitely a lost art. No trip to Denmark would be complete without a stop at the Sorensen Family Clog Museum, where we saw clogs and clog-inspired products like the coffee clogger.

On our way home, we made a stop in Germany for a couple days to visit Baxter's homeland. We stopped in Weezerboden and stayed with some distant cousins, Adolf and Agnes Schmidt. We had a good time looking at old family photos and dining on a delicious meal of sauerkraut stew with turnip ravioli and lots and lots of beer.

We finally made it home and were happy to get back to our day-to-day routine. I have missed several classes at Porter Claymoor's Polka for Dummies classes. Baxter is back to work at Henning's Handy Hideaway, and we picked up the dogs from Miss Paula's Pooch Palace.

I hope you will be by soon to see our pictures. Take care.

Mindy Sandy Freidlander

Dear Midge,

Jeffords and I were out with Tommy and Tabitha Toehill last night and had a wonderful time. We went to Arnie's Amphibian Arena and Italian Cuisine. Tabitha and I had Arnie's famous spaghetti and tofu balls, and the guys had Darcy's homemade lasagna dumplings. We stayed for the 9:00 PM show. Marveline and her dancing frogs were amazing.

Vale Volph and Helen Hettenhausen were the gracious hosts of last week's Ladies of Afton meeting. We learned the art of napkin folding by Estefany Elizondo from Hattozy County. Bernice and Shernice Schwartzman performed a tribute to Ladies president Maxine Monroe. The sisters composed an original song called "Take It to the Max." I had no idea that these ladies were such accomplished accordion players. What talent we have right here in Afton.

While out running errands on Saturday, I managed to stop by at Past Perfect Produce. They sell products just before they go bad, and you can get some pretty good deals. I picked up some slightly brown bananas and some partially mushy pears.

I got dragged into going over to Marco's Lounge with Jobeth Jankowski. We had a few drinks and listened to some great music. One of the highlights was a great song called "If You Stand By Me It Might Rub Off" by Kitty Kasmrichi. She was telling us that the song went number one in Idaho, where it is called "You Might Get Some on You." As we were leaving, we stopped off to say hello to Maybelline Montgomery. She was stunning and sparkly as usual. I swear that woman has never met a rhinestone she did not like. She was there with her husband, the Captain, along with Ferdinand Flemming and his friend Miss Pearl.

I hope you can join us next time.

All the best,
Patty Prouty

Dear Midge,

So good to see you at Ollie Omo's birthday luncheon last Wednesday. You look wonderful. I sure did enjoy the food at Sully's Shamrock Soup Spot. I met the owner, Seamus O'Malley O'Doyle, while we were there and complimented him on his vast assortment of goodies. I had the pickle relish soup, and it was divine.

I wanted to tell you that Sherman finally found a new job. He is going to be the lead shoelacer at Dillinder's Shoe Shack. They only sell lace-up shoes, and they had an opening after Shelby Shiggenstribler retired. I hear she is writing her memoir titled *"All Laced Up and No Place to Go."* They are offering him $4.13 an hour and all the day-old Danish from Feingold's Bakery. How could he not accept with that kind of deal?

I ran into Jojo Johansson at Gnarlstien's Jewelry, and she is full steam ahead with rehearsals for the Greater Afton All-Female Kazoo Band. They are premiering their Spring Cantata at the unveiling of the Harry Cherry memorial plaque at the Friends of San Malandro Falls Park benefit on the eighteenth. I hope we will see you and Reggie. Jojo told me that Karla Koopmann will surely be a standout. She is using her mother's kazoo, and we all know how talented that woman was.

Finally, you have got to try the oatmeal-crusted steak tartare at Wally Wong's. That is the new Asian place that opened up where Dipple's used to be.

Give my love to the family.

Sabrina Sizemore

Dear Midge,

I wanted to tell you that I ran into Kiki Klutsenbaker at the Save the Old Chinchilla Hatchery benefit at Yeager's on Main last Saturday. She, of course, was wearing her chinchilla poncho trimmed in macramé beads and felt triangles. She always knows how to make a fashion statement no matter where she is.

While there I reconnected with Mazee Montooth. She could not wait to tell me about her newest ideas for the upcoming father/daughter dance at St. Audrey the Redeemer Academy. She said that this year's theme is Who's Your Daddy? This year's dance chairwoman, Lydia Lancaster, is excited about the entertainment. Two of Afton's greatest entertainers will grace the stage. Zelda Zazen will present her wonderful cast of hand puppets, including one my favorites, Shaming Shirley. Shirley shames people for little indiscretions like having fourteen items in a ten-items-or-less lane or larger ladies who think they look good in stretch pants. Also appearing is Wade Warbler and his all-tambourine trio, including Imogene Spander and Ida Mae Noxley. They recently returned from playing at the opening ceremonies for the All-State Bricklayers' Rodeo.

The race for the Top Father Award is down to just three finalists. Jerry Mike Lindell, the owner of Krispy Fannies Fried Pies, coaches the junior varsity horseshoe team at the high school and volunteers at the Afton Humane Society, bathing dogs on Saturdays. Finalist number two is Wilbur "Butch" Cranston, who is a vice president at Sinclair Mobile Home Manufacturing. He regularly donates blood to the Mid-America Blood Bank and has been a substitute Portuguese teacher at Jesse James School. Finally, Darnell Dinsmoor, who is a bar back at Tiny's Tavern, cochairs the twelve-step meetings at the Methodist Church. All worthy contenders, and Afton would be proud to have any of them as Top Father this year.

Candy Crankler told me she got her daughter Candy Jr.'s dress for the dance over at Damsel in Dis Dress shop on Clarke Avenue. She said their selection was simply the best she'd seen anywhere. I imagine all the girls will look wonderful.

I hope to see you next week at the annual neighborhood rummage sale.

Betty Claire Rochester

Dear Midge,

I ran in to Pippi LaGranger after church on Sunday. She was there with her brother and his family. They are members of St. Reba at the corner of Millard and Fillmore avenues. That is also where my family goes. She mentioned that you were under the weather, and I hope you are doing much better.

I am counting down the days to the Forty-first Annual Rhubarb Regatta at Lake Wattsatoga in Afton Hills. Hydra Rollins and Kimmy Kilpatrick have been working long hours as cochairs of this year's event. One of the new offerings this year is the Double R Fashion Show and Pie Presentation.

Some of Afton's most notable women will wear designer fashions from Finkman's Fine Frocks and will walk the runway carrying their own homemade rhubarb pie. At the end of the runway, the ladies will strike a pose and present their pie to the distinguished panel of judges.

This year's judges are Sue Sworton of Sue's Sweets in Russellville; Phyllis Pragle, who does a cooking segment on WOOF's *Fabulous Fenton* on channel 12; and Roland Ringhauser, the head chef at Kipper's downtown on the strip.

The regatta will kick off with the always-spectacular boat parade followed by the crowning of Little Miss Rhubarb. I think the sentimental favorite is Argie Andrews. This is her final year to compete, and honestly, if she hadn't failed the third grade several times, she would be out of the running. She has never won, and the whole town is behind her. I hear she really beefed up her talent and now incorporates intermittent birdcalls while reciting the state capitals. This may be her year.

The finale of this year's regatta will be the unveiling of the Rhubarb Pie Best in Show Award, which will be presented by town council president Linus Linder. This year's winner will be featured on the front page of the *Afton Free Press*. The winner will also receive a money order for $177 and a beautiful plaque courtesy of Milan's Miniature Horses and Engraving.

I am sure we will see you and yours at the regatta.

Thinking of you,
Sadie Suzie Slansky

Dear Midge,

I just returned from visiting Joanie Joy Jackson, who is in the hospital at Afton General. She is in for routine tests, and while there, she had her doctor surgically implant false eyelashes. I swear she will do anything in the name of beauty.

Conrad and I ran in to Minerva Morgan while we were at Ansel's Auto Auction on Saturday. She is the bookkeeper there. Our Pinto finally ran its course, and we were in the market for a different car. Conrad wanted something a little sporty, so we settled on a Chevette. It is split-pea green with tinted windows. We are thrilled.

We are thinking of taking the new car when we travel to the Midwest Division Football Classic between the Arnold Anglers and the Topeka Tornados next weekend. We are going with LaWanda and Levi Lewis and Romy and Maury Masterson. It should be a good weekend for football. We like to tailgate while we are there, and I have a big batch of pigs in a blanket ready to go. Instead of the traditional blanket, I like to use cinnamon rolls. It gives it a little kick.

Mark your calendar now for this year's High Heel Hoedown. Two weeks from Friday, ladies from all over the tricounty area will don their high heels and gather for a country-and-Western-themed gala under the big tent at Avery and Ursula Westchester's farm just outside Afton in Bueno Royale Estates. Catering by Gracie Bell Bittsman at Graybell Catering promises to be a culinary delight. This year's entertainment is provided by Drucila Davenport and her band, The Spanking Monkeys.

They just announced that the winner of this year's Golden

High Heel Award is none other than Gladney Gilbert. I am so happy for her. She gives so much back to the community. I heard just this past year that she cleaned her closet and donated hundreds of pairs of high heels to the sisters at St. Beverly the Anointed Convent over in Leamay.

I am sure the nuns are enjoying the new shoes, and it must be quite the difference from their traditional footwear.

I am looking forward to wearing my new Sammie J's red satin pumps with the brass heels to the gala.

Will be glad to see you there, Midge. Take Care.

Harriet Grossman

Dear Mr. and Mrs. Reggie Clovis,

It is with great pleasure that we inform you that you have been selected as a Model American Family by the Center for the Common American. We believe you exemplify the ideal family based on your family unit size, educational background, service to community, and outstanding ideals. We award families based solely on the strict criteria outlined above.

You will be included in our annual publication of *Model American Families* and will be awarded a beautiful certificate suitable for framing to be displayed in your home. We will need to verify a few things and have enclosed a questionnaire for you to fill out and return in the postage-paid envelope. After the verification, we will then photograph your family and interview a few carefully selected family members, friends, and coworkers to offer inspiring testimonials about your family.

The annual publication of *Model American Families* will be published by the good folks at Little Known Press and be sold exclusively through our website, by mail order, or through membership in the Center for the Common American. Each book is bound by an extraordinary leatherette binding with genuine gold leaf imprint. You will be able to purchase a copy for yourself or any family member for the reduced price of $97.98, and all orders from the general public will be at our normal rate of $100. Each is shipped in a deluxe gift box.

Each winning family will have a featured biography, family photo, and testimonials. We limit each year's Model American Family class to just three hundred, and we are so proud that you have been selected. Please be sure to complete the enclosed form and return to us promptly.

We look forward to welcoming you as our next Model American Family.

Sincerely,
Hilary Hixon, President
Center for the Common American Family

~~~~~~

Dear Midge,

Congratulations on your Best in Show win and yet another triumph for the unstoppable Midge Clovis. My entry in the Most Unusual Flower category did not fare so well this year. I was able to cross-pollinate a carnation with a cabbage. I called it Carnage, and the judges passed it by without so much as an honorable mention. But I'm not bitter. There is always next year, and I am already working on my entry.

You seem to be all the buzz, as word has it that you will be appearing on *Fabulous Fenton*. We will be watching, so don't you stumble now.

Irma Pickens

Dear Midge,

Aunt Ona and Uncle Hank mentioned that you were coordinating the Clovis family reunion, and I wanted to offer any help. In years past we have tried to have it in the summer so that we could contain the festivities to an outdoor area; however, Willard and I are not opposed to having it at our house or perhaps we could have it at the Lodge. If we give them enough notice, we can usually reserve the building as long as the Beavers are not having a meeting or event. Seems like Willard is always down there for something. That fool even talked me into getting involved with the women's branch, and now all I seem to do is make food for the gatherings. Some of the other Beaverette's and I get together and play bridge while the guys are out.

This will be the Fiftieth Annual Clovis Calvelcade, and I think we should do it up nice. Some of the older relatives are really getting up there, and it would be nice to salute them in some special way. Good Golly, I think Aunt Lodi, Aunt Mert, Uncle Cleon, Uncle Martel, and Great-Aunt Flossy have been coming to these reunions since they started. Flossie's husband, Mervin, was one of the first Clovis family members to settle in to this area. *He* used to tell some really great stories, and now we are at the mercy of Flossy and the others to remember, and some days that is a real challenge.

Please let me know if I can help in any way and remember our offer to use our house or the Lodge. Call me next week so we can catch up.

Cozy Clovis Weingardt

Dear Midge,

Cousin Cozy called me to say that you are in charge of this year's Clovis family reunion. I think your idea of a talent show to salute Aunt Flossie is a great idea. Flossie's Follies will be a great highlight to our shindig. After all, she deserves something for being the oldest living Clovis.

I talked to Bart and Mabeline, Uncle Hotshot and Aunt Virginia, cousins Marty, Buck, and Wilma, and they will all be there. I even think Aunt Carol and Uncle Cap will be down from Shallow Lake too. I think their son Percy will not be there because of a bout with colitis.

Edison and Helene, Marcus and Serena, and Millard and Aunt Lu will also be there as usual. I think we have a fine line up of talent. Aunt Lu does interpretive dance, Uncle Hotshot blows bubbles from his pipe, Aunt Carol and Uncle Cap do birdcalls, and Wilma can sing the theme song to the *Mary Tyler Moore Show*. Cart and Mabeline are learning the harmonica, so that will be a treat, and I hear Simone is writing a special song for Aunt Flossie. I know it will be great, and if not, Flossie cannot hear a damn thing anyway.

Let me know what I can do.

Tootles,
Geraldine and Frank Clovis

Dear Midge,

It was good to see you at Dr. Snodgrass's office on Thursday. He is one of the best dentists in town. I went for a simple cleaning and ended up having a cavity removed, needing a crown replaced, and three teeth extracted. Those damn dentists—it is no wonder so many people fear them.

Do you know Ulysses Moinsker from Randall's Rickety Shack and Hardware Store? He is a friend of Sal's, and I mentioned to him the problem you are having with those pesky critters. Raccoons can be annoying as you know, and he mentioned several remedies.

First there is Raccoon-B-Gone. It is in pellet form and is sprinkled near the trashcan. The raccoon becomes terribly ill and flees the site.

Second, and most effective, is a trap. Midge, these devices are the size of a microwave oven, and you set the door to slam shut once the little fellow goes to the trap to retrieve the bait.

Finally, there is an experimental technique that has not been used that often around here. Ulysses recommends that this be used with extreme caution. You tranquilize the varmint by shooting a strong and powerful dart from a gun. You'd have to stake out the area they most frequent and be ready, aim, and fire.

Now, Midge, there are some side effects. Just ask Bobby Beasley and his wife, Bernice. The way Bernice tells the story, Bobby had staked out the little monster and had his gun aimed when he slipped and the gun went off. Just so happened the dart entered Bobby's left leg, and he passed out.

When Bobby came to, the raccoons had eaten his sandwich and urinated on him. It was almost as if they were hiding behind trees, laughing at him.

Midge, whatever method you use, please be careful.

Hope to see you again soon.

Dornell

Dear Midge,

Mary Sue Millersville said you were the go-to gal for information on this year's Random Hearts Valentine Gala.

Last year's gala was Isn't it Romantic with DuBose Dunwoody and his three-piece orchestra serenading us with love songs.

I'm not sure what the theme will be this year, but I wanted to throw out a couple slogans.

1. Roses are red, violets blue, why did you wear that ugly shoe.

2. Flowers are a girl's best friend till they die.

3. Happy Valentine's Day, you bitch!

That last one was for the dog lover in all of us. Whatever you choose, Midge, I am certain it will be grand.

I'm looking forward to the special evening. I'm wearing my wedding dress, which I had dyed red just for the occasion.

I am already getting excited to see all the wonderful decorations. I personally think crepe-paper streamers, cutout hearts, and balloons would be perfect. But that is just my little say-so.

Midge, we're looking forward to seeing you and Reggie.

Uvia Ulster-Umstetter

Mrs. Midge Clovis

4494 Rothschild Street

Afton MO 63130

Dear Mrs. Clovis,

My name is Fritz Fordermann, and I am the president of Happy Trails Breakfast Flakes. I wanted to personally write you and congratulate you on your winning entry in our Happy Trails name-our-tagline contest.

Your winning entry, "A happy trail to your tummy, the breakfast flake for your colon," was well received by our judges, and your entry beat out over 150,000 other entries. Job well done, Mrs. Clovis.

As grand-prize winner you will receive a new Ford Tempo, $2,739 in cash, a trip for two anywhere Premier Airlines flies domestically, and a lifetime supply of Happy Trails Breakfast Flakes.

Again my sincere appreciation to you for your ingenious and inspiring slogan. Once again, a hardy congratulations to you on your well-deserved success.

Kindest personal regards,
Fritz Fordermann
President
Gazebo Food Products Inc.

Dear Midge,

It was such a special treat to run into you recently at the charity cakewalk at the Jewish Cultural Center. I am not Jewish, but we light a menorah at Christmas for the heck of it, so I feel like I am connected to the faith.

Madeline Polsky and I were impressed with the array of deserts the event brought in. I, of course, made my pineapple upside-down cake. I use canned pineapple, and I think that makes the difference.

Well, it is Mother's Day this weekend, and Sid's mother is coming in from Albany. I have cleaned for a week and shuffled the kids into other rooms to make way for her visit. She will be here for a week. I think that is a week too long for her nagging, complaining, and antics. She *always* has something wrong with her even if most of it is in her head. And no matter what I say or do, she has done it better in the past.

We are going to the buffet at Wayne's Western Sidekick. The food is good and always pretty fresh, and Edna seems to enjoy it there. Since Sid's father passed away, we try to see her as much as possible, and it is just easier for her to fly out here than for us to pile in the wagon and drive that distance. We did it over Christmas, and it was all I could do from having a breakdown. Sid and I fought the whole time.

I was saddened to hear of the passing of Marvin Jo Johnson. He was such a wonderful and bright spot at Paul's Party Palace, and wedding receptions will no longer be the same without his "Welcome to the PP" when we are there.

Crandel's Casa over in Sturnum burned down. Sid and I

were disappointed when we drove over last week for some nachos. They always did have the best in the tricounty area. Evie Voust told me of a great little sandwich shop going in on the backside of town square. I think she said Mavis and Ina Agnes were opening up MIA Bread Stop around the first of the month.

I noticed that the Little Sisters of Tex Arkansas Convent were having a concert to raise money for a mission trip to Nebraska. I think they plan to minister to the street gangs in Lincoln. They have adopted a new motto, "Get 'em off the street and into jeans that fit, and then they will know Jesus and in the church they'll sit."

I think a group of us are going to the concert and hope that you and Edna Rae will consider joining us.

Let's make it not so long between visits, Midge. We are not getting any younger.

All the best,
Junequelle Orvis

Dear Midge,

I got a note in the mail from Dorothy Tothmansckope. She hosted her bridge club on Saturday. She said she cleaned all week and dug through hundreds of recipes in preparation.

She ended up serving a Jell-O mold with cottage cheese, chips and salsa, chicken fingers, and, for dessert, ice-cream sandwiches.

She ended up having a total of fourteen ladies and said everything was great, except that Agnes Morningstar was in a mood. Agnes did nothing but complain about Smokey all evening.

Ezra and Sheila Lambshed and Anita and Sammy Jake Cooksey joined Arthur and I at Dodi's Diner on Wednesday evening. They have individual jukeboxes on the tables and serve the best patty melt around.

The Lyndhurst twins, Fannie and Flora, just got back from performing their song and dance routine at the Ozark Recreational Arena and Amusement Park. They sang and danced to "The Way We Were." I hear it was amazing.

Slappy Stringman is in the hospital for observation. Late Sunday evening, he was dragged down the street when his snowblower went berserk.

I heard that Trixie Bethpage has lost four pounds with the amazing diet pills called Drop 'Em. They claim ten pounds in ten days, but it has been three weeks for Trixie. I told her not give up and persevere.

I have got to run. See you soon.

Kalli McClusky

~~~~~~~~~~~~~~~~~~~~~~~~~~~~~~~~~~~~~~~

Dear Midge,

It was great to see you at Dixie's Bowling Center Tuesday night. The league is great right now. You sure looked good on the lanes last night. I noticed you bowled a 23, which is an improvement over your 19 a week before. Keep doing this well, and we'll have a run for our money soon.

I love that you've named your team the Slow But Shirleys.

My team consists of Marsha Manchester, Marjorie Wintermuster, Crawford Pigbottom, Jamie Jarvis, Mavis Morrehead, and Tandy Tomlinson. Since we're all approaching a certain age, we've decided to call ourselves The Better Late than Nevers. We're all first-time bowlers too.

Ivan and I just returned from a long weekend in Winehurst Missouri at the Sunshine Trailer Park. While there, we visited the Penguin Park. They are such amazing characters. I told Ivan I wanted one but then thought about how would we transport it home and where we would keep it. Ivan suggested the Deepfreeze in the garage, and I gave him a good talking to about cruelty to animals. The he suggested the bathtub, and I actually thought that was a better idea.

Then I came to my senses. Midge, after all, our dog barely likes us. He'd never go for another animal in the house. He rules the roost.

That's it for now.

June Allenston

Dear Midge,

I wanted to take some time to write and catch up. Last week Beauregard and Eleanor Lamplinger invited a few couples from church over for chicken liver stew, and after digesting our dinner, we sat in the living room over coffee. It was a delightful evening.

Eleanor was telling us of the misfortune her mother encountered recently on her trip to the Yuka Valley area of Ohio. She was riding a horse at the Treadwater Spa and Reserve, and the horse became spooked by a flock of mockingbirds. The horse took off in a hearty gallop, and Eleanor's mother fell off and sprained her wrist and fractured both pinky toes.

She has been helping her mother convalesce for the last two weeks.

Marple and Angie Weavernier were there and were sharing the details of several recent books they read. Angie recently read *The Lust of Lettuce*, a wonderful new book about a young woman's passion for her veggie garden and the price she paid for wanting it all. Marple engaged us in the highlights from *Before Seventy-Six*. It was an interesting tale of the seventy-five years of modern marvels in the city of Partridge, Kentucky. I had no idea that a city with a population of thirteen could be so jam-packed with amazing wonders, such as Otis Cleangazer's collection of hand-painted gumballs and Molly Dilky's collection of amazing photographs of cow teats. I must add a trip to that town to my future travel plans.

I told the story of our neighbors Dredge and Dianna Dohenny. We were all outside talking last Saturday afternoon, when the strangest occurrence took place in the backyard. A flock of nine wild turkeys landed in the yard. There were eight black turkeys and one albino turkey. It was this albino that seemed to be the leader. The turkey moved about in a circle, making strange movements, and the other eight followed exactly doing the same thing. As I struggled to understand this ritual, it dawned on me that these strange birds were doing the chicken dance. It was unbelievable, and had Dredge and Dianna not been there, no one would have ever believed me.

Anyway, Midge, gotta run. Let's have coffee soon.

Best,
Spangela Martin

Dear Midge,

Wanted to let you know we missed you on our theatre trip to New York. It was not the same without you, but we managed to have a little fun. We were all stunned to learn that the gingivitis had spread outside your mouth and down your face. I know you will be better soon.

Marlene, Coco, Ruthie, Toad, and I were tearing up the town from the moment we left our house. We were pleasantly surprised when we were all upgraded to first class on our flight to New York City. The plush seats were oh so nice, and they served us cocktails in actual glasses with warm nuts. Can you imagine the joy we felt? On the way there, Ruthie and Coco had a bit too much to drink and could barely support themselves at the baggage claim. We took cabs to the hotel. Marlene, Ruthie, and I took one cab; and Coco and Toad took another. I am not sure what happened, but their taxi arrived twenty minutes after ours.

We got settled in to our rooms and went down to the lounge for a few more drinks before bed. Marlene met some guy from Brazil, and with that accent, we were all just like butter and lost ourselves in the moment.

The next day it was off to discover the town. The sheer magnitude of it all was a bit overwhelming. We decided we had to see it all. We boarded a sightseeing bus and toured the city. We had the chance to see Times Square, Little Italy, Chinatown, the Empire State Building, Wall Street, and the Statue of Liberty. We ate lunch from one of the street vendors, and although I was cautious, it was mighty good.

Later after freshening up, we went to the first of three

scheduled Broadway shows. We were all decked out in our finest threads. I wore my black floor-length tunic over pants and the glittery shoes I had from Johnny and Sue's twenty-fifth anniversary bash. Coco had on a ball gown from the shrine event, and the others were in the dresses they had from their cruise. We were all overdressed for sure but had so much fun. We almost could not fit Coco and that dress into the same cab, but we managed. We saw *Wicked*. It was a marvelous musical, and the songs were magical. Afterward, we hit every bar we found on our way back to the hotel until Ruthie broke the strap on her dress. She was doing shots at the bar when her dress caught on something and the girls fell out for a scant second. Thank God we found a safety pin.

The next day it was off to do some shopping. We found our way to Chinatown and found the designer knockoffs sold on the street. We did some damage and had to make a trip back to the hotel to drop off our bargains. Later we attended a showing of Naked Guys Singing. Midge, they were right there in front of us with all their glory showing. The songs and dance numbers were great, but all you could do was stare at the nude bodies. It got me thinking about trading Melvin in for a newer and larger model. It was only a thought. The audience was filled with mostly gay men. They were so nice and thought we were all drag queens, which made us feel so beautiful.

Finally on our last day, we decided to head out to Central Park. We walked and walked and did a lot of people watching. Let's just say all the crazies do not live in Afton; New York has its share too. I mean these people are as crazy as Kiki, the lady outside the A&P who quacks like a duck when she sees children. That night we saw *Lion King*, and it was so amazing. We were so glad we opted to see it rather than a second night of naked men.

Another great trip with lots of good food, far too much good drinks, and many good friends. Midge, we will be glad to get you well again so you can join us on our next great adventure to Hollywood. I am hoping to get us tickets to a game show. How much fun would it be to spin the big wheel with Bob Barker? He is older than dirt but easy on the eyes.

Talk soon,
Gloria

Dear Midge,

I hope you are doing well. With all the active weather we've had, there is no telling anymore. Last week we had seventy degrees and then, yesterday, so much snow that I could not see my Impala, and the dog house is buried.

Two weeks ago, I went to the quilt show sponsored by Sanderson's Sewing World and just saw some beautiful quilts. The time and effort put into some of them are just mind-boggling.

I got there just in time to see the winners announced by the judges. They had no small task choosing the top prize, and this year the winner was Shiloh Gomez and her amazing tribute to the fifty states—an outstanding map of the USA with the fifty states in grand glory with the state flower, motto, and then a little something about each one. For instance, on Nebraska, she has a triple hamburger from Littleton's Dunk 'n' Dine (the state's most famous burger joint). In Maine, she has the famous three-headed snake from the Bangor Reptile Museum, and from Utah, she had the world's largest milking cow from the dairy preserve in Provo. This cow stands almost ten feet tall. The udders are quite spectacular.

The judges were Mary Beth Hoedestifly, home economics teacher at the high school; Karen Connelly-Stiffle for the craft consortium; and, finally, Patsy Berhardshiff from Sanderson's. Patsy had some type of Greek goddess dress on with some strange peplum waist and hemline. I could have sworn that I had seen the dress before. It was a beautiful print with lilac flowers and eyelet trim. After I went home, I kept seeing that dress in my head over and over again. It finally hit me where I had seen the print. Midge, I was at the White Sale at Wacker's the week before, and I think Patsy was wearing a twin sheet set. I'll be dammed if she wasn't the picture of high fashion.

She posed for pictures with the other judges and winner. I would have chosen a different shade of lipstick. I'm just saying.

Anyway, I need to run. Bobby and I are about to take the shovels for the garage and start digging for the dog.

Stay warm,
Nancy Sue